A
JACK
STEEL
THRILLER

STEEL
TRUST
PREQUEL

GEOFFREY SAIGN

Books by Geoffrey Saign

Jack Steel Thrillers

Steel Trust

Steel Force

Steel Assassin

Steel Justice

Alex Sight Thrillers

Kill Sight

For all the men and women
who keep our country out of harm's way...

Interior design by Lazar Kackarovski

Printed in the United States of America
ISBN-13: 978-1-079549-16-4

BEFORE YOU GET STARTED...

Dear Reader,

I hope you enjoy getting to know how Jack Steel got his start. This prequel gives you a roadmap for Jack's state of mind at the beginning of *Steel Force*, Book 1 of the Jack Steel Thriller series. An excerpt of *Steel Force* is at the end of this book.

I hope you enjoy the ride!

Best,

Geoffrey Saign

https://geoffreysaign.net

"Love begins by taking care of the closest ones—the ones at home."

~ Mother Teresa ~
(1910–1997)

PROLOGUE

BILL SMILED AS HE watched his ten-year-old daughter, Lydia. She carried a small daypack and was working hard to keep up with his wife, who was ahead of her. Lydia was determined to make it to the lake, her long brown hair bouncing with her steps. Her grandfather had told her it was a long hike and Lydia had said she still wanted to do it. Bill admired his daughter's spirit.

The woods were alive with woodpeckers hammering trees and cardinals singing, and the late morning July sun shone through the tall pine and birch trees. Another beautiful day in Canadian wilderness. Bill was thankful he had chosen shorts and a T-shirt for the building heat.

Today was their second day in the forest, and his wife's father, Frank, had suggested a hike from their campsite to see a small lake and do a little fishing. There were no groomed trails, but Frank had been camping and hiking up here all his life and had assured them it was safe. For sixty-five, the man was robust, healthy, and the consummate outdoorsman. Bill trusted him, but he hadn't wanted to do the long hike. However his wife and daughter had both said they wanted to see the lake, so he had been outvoted. He didn't mind. Seeing his daughter and wife happy made him content.

After three hours of hiking through the forest they arrived at the lake, sweaty, hot, and ready for a break. Bill was glad they had come. The water shone like a blue jewel nestled amid surrounding pine, and sunshine sparkled on the water.

They walked up to the shoreline, where a short strip of sand and rocks provided a narrow beach. Lydia smiled, took off her daypack, and walked up to the water with her grandfather.

Bill sighed as he stood by his wife, Jan. She nudged him with her shoulder and beamed at him. Taking the hint, he leaned over and kissed her, and then held her.

"Thanks for being a good sport, honey," she said softly.

"It was worth the effort." As he gazed over her shoulder, south along the lakeshore, he saw a small cabin. Frank had said it had been grandfathered into the provincial park but he didn't think anyone used it anymore.

As Bill stared, three men walked out of the cabin onto the small front open deck. One of the men looked his way. The man was carrying something on his shoulder, and when Bill recognized it his mouth became dry. It looked like a large gun on a carry strap.

"We have to leave, Jan." He pulled back from his wife, and grabbed her elbow, looking for his daughter.

"Why, Bill? What's wrong?"

Frank was already walking away from the lake with Lydia, holding her hand and carrying her daypack in his other hand.

"Why do we have to leave, Grandpa?" Lydia's voice betrayed obvious disappointment, but she didn't resist.

Frank's face was taut, and he barely paused as he said to Bill and Jan, "Turn around, don't run, walk, don't talk."

"What's going on?" Jan's brow was knit.

Frank said tersely, "The men at the cabin have a machine gun, and we're going to err on the side of caution. Let's go." He hurried into the forest with Lydia.

Bill squeezed his wife's shoulder and guided her to follow Frank. Jan's lips pursed, but she walked briskly ahead of him.

As soon as they entered the forest and the cabin was blocked by trees, Frank said softly, "Run!"

Frank had a belly, but he still led them in an easy gait, Lydia behind him, Jan third, Bill last. Bill felt his heart pound as he ran over the soft ground on his tennis shoes, weaving around trees. They were all in reasonable shape, and Bill hoped the men on the porch assumed they had not seen the gun, or didn't care if they had.

Jan glanced back at him several times, her face strained. He tried to appear calm and gave her small encouraging smiles.

Every few minutes he glanced over his shoulder to see if he was being followed, each time relieved to see no one there. His thoughts raced over what men were doing in the wilderness with that kind of weapon. Maybe just shooting practice or even hunting. Maybe poachers. But Frank knew his weapons and wouldn't have bolted if the gun was used for hunting. Other ideas came up that Bill didn't want to consider.

After a quarter mile Frank stopped abruptly. Lydia stopped behind him, and Jan ended up beside her daughter, putting her arm around Lydia's shoulders.

Bill halted behind his wife, his gaze frozen on the figure ahead of Frank.

A man stood partially hidden behind a tree, aiming a pistol at them. The man's stance looked relaxed, but his eyes were narrowed.

Bill remained behind his wife, wondering if just one man had come after them. He had a cell phone, but the reception wasn't great up here. He quietly pulled it out of his pocket, his action hidden by his wife's body. Glancing down at the phone, he decided to risk calling 911. He muted all the sounds in settings in seconds, and then tapped 91—a gunshot behind him startled him, and then he collapsed to the ground, landing softly with dirt and pine needles near his mouth.

He felt something sticky spreading across his chest. From the ground he was aware of his wife turning around, gasping, her face taut and pale. Lydia screamed.

Someone else was taking the phone from his hand.

Then he lost consciousness.

CHAPTER 1

Op: HELLFIRE

MAJOR JACK STEEL STEPPED off the plane and onto the tarmac, his thoughts turning to three terrorists he had to kill.

He immediately slipped his black Lycra hood over his head so only his eyes and mouth were visible. A Jeep pulled up beside him. He got into the front passenger seat and ignored the driver, who did the same to him. The sun had already set, but the late July heat felt good.

They stopped at a two-prop amphibious seaplane, where he climbed the steps to a rear passenger seat and buckled in.

He needed a clear head so he allowed Carol's words to float through him once more: *You promised to quit after Afghanistan. Your daughter needs you. I need you. We should be your priority. You need to choose.*

Carol and his daughter Rachel were disappointed that he had left on another Op six months after returning from Afghanistan. He couldn't tell them that he had been asked to leave Army Special Forces to secretly enroll in the newly-formed Blackhood Ops.

However he didn't think he needed to choose family over Ops. They both mattered. And Blackhood didn't put his family at risk—eliminating terrorist threats made Carol and Rachel safer. Satisfied with his logic, he let it go and closed his eyes to get some rest.

An hour later the copilot said, "Get ready. Twenty minutes."

On the floor was a large duffel bag. Steel unzipped it. From it he retrieved a sheathed Ka-Bar seven-inch fixed blade knife—he liked the leather handle—and attached the sheath to his belt.

Next he pulled out a Glock 19 with attached suppressor and side holster, along with a SIG MCX Rattler—the rifle-caliber machine gun had a red dot sight, suppressor, and carry strap. Its folding stock and short barrel made it easy to conceal. Both guns had their serial numbers filed off.

He put on the hip holster and slung the Rattler carry strap over his head. He also had a Benchmade 3300BK Infidel auto OTF blade in a horizontal belt-sheath against his back, beneath his untucked flannel shirt.

Lastly he pulled out a medium-sized waterproof sling bag made of tough Cordura, which he also looped over his head. He quickly slipped into the harness of his square parachute and slid open the side door. The night air was cool. He was glad he had a waterproof windbreaker over his flannel shirt. His jeans kept his legs warm.

In a minute the copilot said, "Go."

He jumped.

Waiting only a few seconds, he pulled the rip cord. The chute opened softly with a small tug on his harness. The moonlight allowed him to see the water shimmering below. Using the steering lines, he aimed toward a narrow beach at the eastern edge of the lake.

As he neared his destination he noted the wind was out of the north. He steered into it, slowing his forward motion. The fresh scent of lake water drifted up to him.

In a minute he landed on his hiking boots, walking forward with relative ease. He yanked on a line to collapse the chute. Working fast, he bunched it up and carried it to the tree line where he covered it with brush and sticks. He would retrieve it when the boat came for the extraction at midnight the following day.

He unzipped the sling bag. Its inner pockets held beef jerky and protein bars, a compass, canteen, small flashlight, binoculars, heavy-duty black zip ties, night vision monocular, first aid kit, and two spare mags for each gun.

He also had a small battery-operated wireless radio, a throat mike, and an earpiece. No long-range radio or sat phone.

The U.S. government didn't want an international crisis with an ally so they would be communication silent. And given the low-tech nature of the impending terrorist attack, there would be no real-time tracking with drones or satellites. For security, the general running Blackhood Ops didn't want any record anyway, preferring to minimize the number of personnel who knew about the Op.

He slid the mike around his neck, attached the earpiece, and pocketed the small radio.

Before he left home he had memorized the target location and the rendezvous point. The other two men had come in from different areas of the country. Colonel Danker had been ordered to restrict the number of operatives to three since they were in Canada. Blackhood also believed the targets were not highly trained.

Steel estimated he had two klicks to reach the rendezvous point.

He lined up the compass and walked into the birch and pine trees. Looping the canteen over his head along with the sling bag, he kept the moon over his left shoulder. The ground was soft beneath his boots, his pace constant over low hills and through gullies.

In the distance a northern saw-whet owl gave its high-pitched *too-too-too*. He paused to listen. Otherwise the forest was quiet, calming him. He had a deep abiding love of wildlife and nature.

He also loved the night. Moving in the dark was second nature to him after caving for decades. That ability often provided another advantage over the enemy.

Colonel Danker had briefed him early in the morning to lead the first Blackhood Op in hurry-up status, which had left him little time to prepare with his virtual reality program. The military had developed the VR program to increase Blackhood operatives' skill development. He had used it obsessively for six months to hone his elite skills developed in martial arts, Special Forces, and Delta Force.

He practiced using a full-body haptic suit—including boots, gloves, a headpiece, and goggles. The VR program could simulate inclines, uneven ground, temperature shifts, pain, and any kind of fighting he might encounter with either hand to hand or weapon scenarios.

He loved the program and had convinced his superiors to allow him to install it in his barn. It gave him a level of preparedness that he had never thought possible.

His thoughts turned to the mission. An ISIS splinter group had recruited three Canadians to cross the border into Minnesota. Colonel Danker had said intel indicated the terrorists intended to use pipe bombs to hit random crowded areas or cause train derailments. Blackhood analysts believed the suspects would be supplied with munitions in Minnesota.

Steel had listened to Danker, imagining Carol and Rachel in their favorite restaurant for breakfast, ending up bloodied or dead. He wouldn't allow these men to bring that kind of chaos to his country.

Blackhood Ops had tracked the three suspected terrorists during overseas trips, where it was believed they made contact with the ISIS splinter group.

Still, Canada didn't agree that the intel was solid enough for an arrest and refused to incarcerate the men—especially since the three suspects were Canadian citizens without any criminal or military background. In addition, since ISIS had been largely routed out of Iraq, many countries viewed the terrorist organization as less of a threat.

Even if Canada arrested the suspects, Blackhood Ops determined that the charges would be dropped based on lack of evidence. Meanwhile Blackhood had learned the trio were on their way to a remote cabin owned by one of the suspects. The cabin wasn't far from the U.S. border.

The highly classified Blackhood Ops charter gave the President permission to terminate suspected terrorists on foreign soil if they posed an imminent threat and couldn't be brought to a successful closed trial. Thus he had signed off on the covert mission.

In a half-hour Steel reached a river. He followed it fifty yards south and stopped, waiting.

In a minute a small flashlight blinked three times ahead of him. Digging out his flashlight, he gave three blinks back. One blink returned. He gave two blinks in response. The signals had been prearranged to exclude any possibility of one of them being captured and someone else using the radio.

He still approached the destination carefully, moving from tree to tree until he saw two men standing on the shore of the river beside a canoe. They both wore similar Lycra hoods.

Blackhood operatives weren't allowed to see each other's faces or share any personal information or names. They also were not allowed to make contact during an Op with anyone except their fellow operatives. Steel appreciated the precautions because they helped maintain Op secrecy and protected the operatives.

Walking in closer, he stopped twenty feet away, studying them both carefully. He gave his call sign. "Al." He gave the Op name next, which also served as the code name. "Hellfire."

The stocky man answered first, his voice calm and steady. "Brad."

Brad was a few inches shorter than Steel's six-two frame and also wore jeans and a drab green pullover beneath a hooded rain jacket. Maybe forty. He was second in command, should things go south.

Brad pointed to the other man. "Charlie."

Wiry and a bit taller than Steel, Charlie wore black jeans and a dark green plaid flannel shirt beneath a black jacket.

Sounding as if he was in his late twenties, he lifted his chin in acknowledgment and said, "Sir."

Brad had a Rattler slung over his shoulder, but Charlie had a silenced HK416 carbine fitted with a holographic laser sight. Holographic sights had high accuracy, but a shorter battery life than a red dot—still adequate for a one-day mission. They both had Glocks, knives, sling bags, throat mikes, and earpieces.

"How long have you been waiting?" asked Steel.

"An hour," said Brad. "What's the plan?"

"Cross the river and walk east three hours before we camp."

They pushed the canoe out, got in, and paddled across, watching the far bank carefully.

Steel was in the stern, scanning the opposite shoreline. His daughter, Rachel, would love a night hike and paddle like this. He resolved to take her and Carol to a cabin when he returned home.

After crossing sixty yards of water, they beached the canoe and pulled it up on shore to hide it. They were now in Canada. Steel checked the compass and moon, and then led the others east.

Thirty minutes later soft sounds to the north startled him. He dropped to his knees behind a tree with the others. Charlie and Brad immediately had their guns up. Steel noted Brad's steady grip on his weapon and his relaxed breathing, while Charlie regripped his gun.

Using the night vision monocular, Steel scanned north. "Black bears," he whispered.

A mother and two cubs. He enjoyed watching them, glad to see them move off farther north. He mentally played out several scenarios of the bears blundering into their path on the way out. Not a problem. But they would have to be alert. Rising, he continued hiking.

After another two and a half hours he found a suitable clump of trees for camp.

He motioned to the others. "Brad, you and Charlie get some rest. I'll take first watch, Brad second. We leave before dawn."

Both men moved toward a tree to unpack and sleep.

Steel found a tree to sit against, placing the guns beside him on the moss-covered ground. The north side of the tree had more moss on it—typical due to less sunshine hitting it.

By his calculations they were four hours south of the target cabin. Blackhood wasn't sure of the terrorists' entry point into Minnesota. Due south made the most sense but wasn't a given.

He had to silence concerns about not knowing who he was working with. Brad moved with practiced strides, held his weapon with confidence, and scanned his surroundings continually. Charlie seemed more reactive—which could be a problem in a tense situation. But Colonel Danker had insisted both men were highly skilled.

He drank some water. Brad relieved him in a few hours to take watch.

Steel fell asleep in minutes.

He woke to movement on his left. Charlie was a dark figure squatting down by his gear. Time to go. He stretched, drank water, and chewed jerky. In minutes he finished and put his palm on his head, signaling *On me*.

Brad was kneeling, readying his gear, and he stood and stepped close to Steel. Charlie quickly joined them.

Steel talked tersely. "We hike north for eight klicks. The three targets are at an isolated cabin on a lake. All males, mid-to-late twenties. We'll assess strategy when we arrive. Intel suggests they'll have small arms and plan to acquire more weapons once they cross the border. We want to take at least one of them alive for interrogation. Termination follows. No one else is expected to be there. Noncombatants are expendable if they support the terrorists or threaten mission success. Questions?"

Charlie and Brad remained silent.

Steel nodded. "Brad, you take point. I'll bring up the rear."

Brad turned and led them into the woods at a steady pace.

Steel followed Charlie, preferring to keep both men ahead of him. He wanted to make sure they weren't followed. That seemed unlikely, but he had learned long ago to expect the unexpected.

As dawn approached, the forest slowly awoke. Cardinal songs and blue jay cries broke the silence, along with crows cawing among the spruce and aspen trees. A northern flicker pounded a trunk in the distance and the scent of pine filled the air. Normally Steel would stop to enjoy the beauty. All of it had a peaceful quality, at odds with the mission he was leading.

Brad kept a brisk pace through the trees for several hours. When he stopped, he held up a hand and whispered into his mike, "Lake just ahead, cabin visible to our west."

Steel didn't want to be spotted by anyone in the cabin. "Circle west to a hundred yards from the rear door."

"Roger that."

Brad led them for another ten minutes at a fast pace to the northwest, stopping at the bottom of a forty-five-degree incline of twenty feet. He raised a hand.

Charlie stopped and surveyed the eastern terrain, while Steel walked past him and Brad. Gripping the Rattler, Steel continued a dozen yards and knelt to survey the forest to the north.

Brad crouched and hustled up the hill, stopping near the top. In one smooth motion he went down to his knees, and then his belly, slowly crawling out of sight over the top of the hill.

In a minute Brad's voice came through their earpieces. "Cabin just ahead. Back door facing west with two small rear windows. No targets visible. There's a trip-wire attached to a claymore a few feet ahead of me."

Steel didn't like it. The claymore suggested the terrorists wanted to guarantee there were no surprise attacks. They were waiting for something. He discarded the Blackhood intel that the terrorists were just amateurs recruited for random acts of violence in the U.S. The claymore suggested something bigger was at stake.

He quickly ran through options in his head, keeping his voice a whisper. "Brad, signal when the claymore is cleared, eyes on the back door. Charlie, after Brad signals, head east to the lake. I'll take north. We'll come in from all three directions. Watch for trip-wires and command-activated claymores closer in. Give the cabin a wide perimeter. Charlie and I on the front door. Brad, the back door."

Charlie nodded, and Brad responded with, "Roger that."

Steel strode another ten yards north, surveying the forest, while keeping an eye on the top of the hill. Charlie walked ten yards east and took a knee, slowly swinging his gun along his sightline.

In a minute Brad's voice came through Steel's earpiece; "Claymore secured."

Steel watched Charlie walk east, and he strode north.

A loud *whomp!* split the air.

CHAPTER 2

S TEEL FLINCHED AND STOPPED, recognizing the sound of a claymore.

The forest turned silent.

Charlie froze. Steel pointed to him and then up the hill.

Charlie crept up the incline, on his belly at the top. He turned to Steel and shook his head, circling his face with a finger and drawing the same finger across the front of his neck.

Steel shoved down his distress over losing his best man. Also the terrorists would be alerted now. He pumped a fist up and down and pointed due east—which should take Charlie outside any claymore trip-wires and get him to the lake to cover any attempted escape.

Charlie took off running.

Steel bolted northwest in a crouch, moving fast while keeping a wide distance from the cabin. Brad must have triggered a second claymore. There was a good chance his body was visible from the cabin. He hoped the terrorists hadn't set explosives farther out.

He wove in and out of trees. The forest still blocked his view of the cabin but moving closer would risk repeating Brad's fate. Climbing a tree also increased the odds of getting shot.

He assumed the terrorists would try to escape in a preplanned action. It was something he had already played out many times in his head.

Charlie needed to arrive at the lake fast enough to cut off any escape by boat. The enemy wouldn't know how many men were coming at them from the rear of the cabin so they wouldn't be eager to make a run west. If he had to pick an exit strategy, it would be by boat first, and as a backup send someone north or south along the lake shoreline—maybe both at once.

A boat motor started up.

"Charlie?" he whispered.

A rifle report reached him, quickly followed by Charlie's voice in the earpiece, "One target down. No others visible."

"Hold your position." Steel ran in a crouch, veering due east, estimating he was still far enough from the perimeter Brad had broken. It took him less than a minute to reach the trees bordering the lakeshore.

A small fishing boat with an idling outboard was floating a hundred yards out on the lake. Barely moving. A man sat slumped over near the engine and appeared dead. Charlie wouldn't have risked a wounded man escaping and must have put a bullet in his head. It gave Steel more confidence in him.

He didn't think anyone could have slipped past him up the shoreline. Still, to be sure he dug out the binoculars and scanned the strip of sand next to the water, looking for any sign of footprints or broken brush. Nothing.

He looked south. The edges of the cabin were visible through the branches and leaves. No windows in the north wall. A hint of movement caught his eye. He peered through the binoculars. A figure was running north along the shoreline.

He whispered, "One target fleeing north. Hold your position and eyes on the back of the cabin."

"Roger that."

He ducked down, set the Rattler on the ground, and pulled the Glock.

Scrambling, he moved to within a dozen yards of the shoreline, stopping behind a big pine. He grabbed a hand-sized rock. With one terrorist dead, he couldn't afford to kill this man right away. Now more than ever they needed to verify the terrorists' plans.

He listened for soft footfalls. Even though he only had a glimpse, he knew the man held a machine gun in his right hand—it looked like a FN P90. That also ruled out amateurs. P90s had armor piercing fifty-round magazines and were illegal for civilians to own.

The man ran past him in a steady pace at the water's edge, wearing a gray sweatshirt, jeans, and tennis shoes. Wiry and fit. A smooth runner.

Steel tossed the rock high and out over the lake twenty feet from the shoreline. Leveling the Glock, he strode out of the forest, picking his steps carefully to avoid making noise.

The rock hit the water with a loud *thunk!*

The terrorist stopped and whirled to face the lake, his P90 leveled.

Steel was already running by the time the man figured it out and turned. Crashing into him from the side, Steel allowed his weight and momentum to topple the terrorist to the ground. The man's gun arm flopped wide.

Steel put a foot on the terrorist's neck, the muzzle of his silenced gun close to his forehead. "Drop the gun, stay quiet, or die."

The man's eyes widened and he released his gun. In his early twenties, the man had curly dark hair and was light-skinned. Steel recognized him from one of the three photos Colonel Danker had shown him. The man reacted like an amateur. Frightened and cooperative. Which didn't fit the profile of a serious terrorist threat.

Steel said, "Turn over, clasp your hands behind your back, and look north. If you lift your head or move your feet or hands, I'll shoot your legs."

The man complied.

Steel stepped to the side and grabbed the man's weapon. He used zip ties to secure the terrorist's wrists and ankles. Satisfied, he walked into the water, looking south with the binoculars.

The cabin sat fifty feet from the water's edge on a short peninsula that jutted out past the lake's northern shore. They couldn't see him from the front windows. An open front porch, two feet off the ground with no railings, was partially visible.

He scanned behind the cabin. Through the trees he caught glimpses of a grassy area. To the south past the cabin he spotted Charlie kneeling behind a large tree near the shoreline, also staring at him with binoculars. He lowered his and said, "Hostile in possession. Continue holding."

"Roger that."

Steel hustled back to his captive and cut the man's ankle zip tie. "Get up and walk into the trees."

He herded the terrorist into the woods, where he ordered the man to lie down on his stomach. Using zip ties, he again secured the terrorist's ankles, and then bent the man's legs so he could fasten another zip tie around each wrist and one ankle.

He hurriedly searched the terrorist and found a wallet with four hundred U.S. dollars and a Minnesota driver's license. Had to be forged. Another pocket yielded a cell phone. On it he found three stored phone numbers.

The area codes were for Minnesota numbers. Three people to contact. For what? Bombs? Memorizing the numbers, he pocketed the phone.

He stared again at the terrorist, whose eyes betrayed fear. He decided to allow himself one minute. Shoving the Glock into the back of the man's thigh, he said tersely, "Tell me what the three U.S. phone contacts are holding for you. Nod your head if you're ready to talk."

The man didn't respond.

Steel tilted the gun so he would avoid arteries and veins, and pulled the trigger, scoring the side of the man's thigh. The terrorist jerked his leg, groaning fiercely, his jeans darkening against his skin and his eyes now wide with fear.

Steel knelt on the man's thigh and this time shoved the Glock between his legs. "This time you're losing your manhood. What are they holding for you in Minnesota?"

The man nodded.

Steel pulled the gag off his mouth, keeping the gun barrel pressed into the man's nether regions. "If I don't like or believe your answer, I'm firing."

"Don't, please," gasped the man. "I'll tell you."

"What is it?"

The man groaned. "Chemicals."

"What kind?"

"Liquid VX. Three barrels."

Steel stared at the man as he adjusted to the much more serious threat. He doubted any terrorist would lie about VX when they could just as easily admit to a lesser crime. And he didn't detect anything in the man's face or voice that indicated a lie. The easy confession also fit his assessment of the man's amateur status. "To use where?"

"Small lakes, city drinking water."

"Why are you waiting here?"

"Confirmation that the barrels have arrived. They were late. The less time we spend in Minnesota the better."

Steel grimaced, imagining screaming children coming out of a swimming lake and dying on the beach. Odorless and tasteless, VX was deadly in small quantities and classified as a weapon of mass destruction. Three barrels could kill millions if put into drinking water—or cause a massive health crisis. Even small amounts on the skin were lethal.

Kim Jong-nam, the estranged half-brother of North Korean leader Kim Jong-un, was murdered when a cloth soaked with VX was rubbed against his face. North Korea had probably supplied the terrorists with the VX. Steel guessed it was a way for North Korea to retaliate against U.S. sanctions without risk.

The potential environmental and wildlife impact bothered him as much as the threat to civilians. If put into lakes the chemical could kill fish, waterfowl, and any wildlife drinking the water.

He pulled out the terrorist's phone and checked the battery. Almost dead. They had to have hiked in here and the cabin wouldn't have electricity. They also hadn't planned on a delay.

He debated calling Colonel Danker. Against protocol. But the VX worried him. He punched the number. No juice. He clenched his jaw.

The man's lips twitched. A nervous tic.

Steel kept the gun pushed into the man's crotch. "What aren't you telling me?"

The man paled. "We have hostages."

He frowned. That made no sense. "How many?"

"Four."

"Why take hostages?"

The man groaned again. "They were hiking nearby and saw us with a machine gun."

It didn't look like the man was lying. If true, that made everything more complicated. He considered his options for approaching the cabin. The terrorists could have set up command-activated claymores along the beach. He assumed the woods were also a risk.

"What's your role?" asked Steel.

"Guide them south to a boat so they can cross the river."

"Without you they can't make it across?"

The man shook his head, looking fearfully at Steel. "They won't be able to find the boat."

"Where are you planning to cross the river?"

"Due south."

"Where are the other claymores?"

"I didn't set them up."

Steel stood up. There wasn't anything else he needed from the man and he couldn't risk this terrorist staying alive. He shot him in the head.

He hustled away, dropping the P90 in a bush and returning to collect his Rattler. Holstering the Glock, he whispered, "Get all that, Charlie?"

"Roger that."

He unfolded the stock on the Rattler and ran out across the shoreline, stopping in an inch of water. From that position he was even with the open front porch. Walking south, he aimed his weapon at the cabin.

Every dozen yards he used the binoculars to check behind the cabin. He also scanned the shoreline to see if he could spot any claymores. Looking south, he spotted Charlie still holding his position close to the shoreline.

Halfway to the cabin he asked, "Any south-facing windows?"

"Negative," answered Charlie.

"Approach in the water in case claymores are set."

Charlie quickly walked into shallow water too, his rifle shouldered and aimed at the cabin. The cabin peninsula allowed Charlie to approach from an angle, like Steel, which made it impossible for anyone to get a shot at him from inside the cabin. They had to hope no claymores were set in front of the cabin.

Steel prepared himself. The remaining terrorist had limited options. The man would be able to see if anyone approached from the rear of the cabin, but he wouldn't know if anyone was hiding in the forest.

The front cabin door opened.

Steel stopped, raising the Rattler.

Charlie stopped too, aiming his rifle at the door.

CHAPTER 3

A MAN WITH A WHITE beard stepped into the doorway, arms raised. Appearing about sixty, he wore jeans and suspenders over a red flannel shirt. Overweight but robust. Steel assumed the man was one of the hostages.

The man looked right and left nearly a hundred-eighty-degrees, from Charlie to Steel, and called out in a shaky voice, "I'm unarmed! I'm unarmed!" Then he lowered his head, as if listening to someone.

Steel couldn't hear the words, but assumed the terrorist was using the hostage to find out his and Charlie's position.

The bearded man lifted his head. "He wants me to tell you that he'll kill me, my daughter, and my ten-year-old granddaughter if you don't back off." He swung his gaze from Charlie to Steel. "He wants you to know that he has explosives and he's not afraid to use them. I believe him. He'll kill all of us. They killed my son-in-law when they grabbed us."

Steel clenched his jaw. The mention of the ten-year-old girl wrenched his gut. It reminded him of Rachel.

Charlie continued moving closer to the cabin until Steel said, "Hold, Charlie."

Charlie stopped, keeping his weapon aimed at the old man.

Steel called out, "Tell the man to come out, unarmed, if he wants to live."

The older man grunted and arched his torso as if something had been shoved into his back. "He's going to kill me, then my daughter and granddaughter. He wants you to retreat or I'm dead."

Steel hesitated.

A shot sounded, followed by a child's shriek. The older man toppled face forward onto the porch. Steel swore and sprinted through the shallow water, his gun aimed at the open door.

Charlie moved out into knee-deep water and began shooting.

Steel couldn't see the windows, but he heard glass breaking. He couldn't take a shot unless he moved farther out into deeper water too. Deciding to keep an eye on the area behind the cabin, he maintained his current approach angle.

A woman cried out, crawling out the door on all fours and stopping to kneel by the body.

Steel halted fifteen feet from the front porch and whispered, "Cease-fire, Charlie."

Keeping his weapon up, Charlie quickly moved laterally back to shallow water so he wasn't a target.

Appearing about thirty and lean, the woman wore a blue blouse and jeans. She sobbed and placed a hand on the back of the dead man. Steel guessed it was her father, and she had already lost her husband. He could hear a child yelling inside the cabin—which abruptly stopped. It spiked his adrenaline further, but he calmed himself by slowing his breathing.

The woman slowly got to her feet and looked at him, and then Charlie. She wiped her eyes and said angrily, "They're going to kill me next, and then my daughter. Please!" Her voice broke and she said, "Please, just back away."

"All right!" Retreating would yield no advantage. He whispered to Charlie, "Get ready to move in." Then louder, "We're listening."

Another shot rang out and the woman collapsed beside her father.

"Damn you!" Steel said under his breath. He rushed forward, glad to see Charlie also running.

He was concerned the terrorist would kill the girl, but he had to push that thought aside. This wasn't his daughter Rachel, and if he didn't focus he would get himself and Charlie killed.

As he neared the cabin, pine trees along the side of it blocked visibility of the back.

They reached the front corners of the cabin at the same time. Steel climbed onto the two-foot-high porch first, while Charlie covered the doorway. Then he covered for Charlie.

Narrow, shot-out windows were on either side of the front door. Curtains hid what was inside. Both windows were centered between the corners of the cabin and the door, four feet above the porch.

The bodies lay in front of the door, which was now closed. Steel gripped his gun, anger choking his throat for a moment. He didn't hear the girl. Maybe she was already dead. The terrorist might be bolting out the back. He was also wary of the terrorist setting a claymore inside the cabin facing the front door.

Charlie glanced at him.

Steel pointed to himself and Charlie, and then drew an outline of a rectangle in the air to signal the windows, and then pointed at himself and then the door. They would both shoot into the windows, then Steel planned to duck the window near him, boot the door, and enter.

Charlie nodded.

He was about to step out to fire, when he heard a soft scrape. Whirling, he glimpsed a large bald man rounding the corner of the cabin, carrying a pistol. Using his nearest leg, Steel spontaneously kicked the man's gun arm into the cabin wall— he didn't have time to bring his gun around.

The terrorist fired, missing Steel, but grabbed his arm and yanked him off the porch.

Steel leapt with the man's pull, trying to land on him, but the terrorist twisted and Steel hit the ground face first, hard. Another gun burst sounded from across the porch. He let go of the Rattler—there was no way to lift it up quickly—and rolled to his side, kicking at the pistol in the man's hand, knocking it away.

The man kicked him in the chest.

Steel grunted, sat up, and rammed a fist at the man's groin, partially connecting. Gasping, the man fell forward, his weight driving Steel into the ground. Pushing a meaty hand against Steel's face, the man ground the back of Steel's head into the dirt, while Steel grabbed the man's pistol arm.

The man's gun fired near Steel's head. Ears ringing, he frantically struck the terrorist with rigid fingers in the front of his neck.

Toppling to the side, the man crawled toward the front edge of the porch.

Steel grabbed his Rattler as bullets bit the edge of the porch. Remaining low, he scrambled to the side of the cabin. The big man had crawled out of sight in front of the deck. Steel peeked around the corner.

A slender dark-haired man holding a FN P90 was stepping over Charlie—who lay prone on the porch.

Steel jerked back as bullets hit the corner of the cabin near him. When the shooting stopped, he angled his gun around the corner and fired a spray of bullets, aiming high and hoping to hit the terrorist without hitting Charlie.

He pulled his gun back. Silence. He peered around the corner. Charlie was the only one visible. The terrorist must have flung himself off the front of the deck.

Steel figured he had seconds before one of the two terrorists fired on him from the front corner of the porch. He needed cover. Ducking through pine trees, he ran toward the back corner of the cabin.

Bullets chewed the trees around him, forcing him to run around the corner without hesitation. Something hard hit him in the forehead and he collapsed.

CHAPTER 4

RACHEL STOOD BEFORE HIM, *wearing her white shorts and red tee, her hands on her hips, her long auburn hair in disarray. Disappointment was etched into her eyes. He had promised to do the chute cave with her when she was more experienced, but now he had to leave and didn't know if he would be coming back...*

When he came out of the dream, Steel had a headache and his ears were still ringing—but not as loud as before. It took him a few seconds to shake off the guilt he had dredged up in the dream. He heard voices but still felt groggy. He kept his head down to listen and observe without signaling that he was awake.

He was sitting against a wall, his ankles zip-tied and his wrists bound behind his back. They had used his zip ties. His chest ached where the big man had kicked him. They had also removed his hood.

He felt for the sheathed OTF knife on the inside of his belt beneath his shirt. Still there.

He peeked sideways. Charlie was sitting a few feet to his left, blood on the front of his jacket near his left shoulder. Charlie's head rested on his chest so Steel couldn't tell if he was alive, but he was zip-tied with his hood also removed.

He grimaced. He prided himself on choosing successful strategies, yet his tactics to assault the cabin would result in Charlie's death. A price he was going to have to pay too.

The idea of not returning to Carol and Rachel was harder to swallow. His obsession with protecting the innocent—a value he had mirrored from his career-military father—would ruin a good life, turning it into shambles for his wife and daughter.

He imagined Rachel's face upon hearing he was dead. He had never let her do caves alone, even easy ones, and he worried how his death would affect her self-confidence. For a moment he also wondered how he had assumed his family was worth the risk of the Op. Suddenly he acutely understood Carol's perception that he should put his family first.

He took several deep breaths and buried his concerns. They hadn't killed him yet so he had a chance.

His daily virtual reality training was built around defeating the Kobayashi Maru test principle. He believed there was always a way out of seemingly impossible situations and used the VR training to practice endless variations to hone skill sets for Ops. He also had excellent improvisational skills.

Thus he focused on his own advice when a plan went bad; *Stay calm, assess options, look for a solution.*

He snuck a quick glance up.

Four terrorists sat around the table, murmuring in Arabic. Six terrorists in total, not three. His dead captive had omitted that fact. His ringing ears didn't pick up everything, but he knew a fair amount of the language. They were talking about leaving soon.

The large man he had fought resembled the photograph Danker had shown him of the Albanian. He appeared solid, dependable, but not the brains behind this group. The other three men had been missing from Danker's photos. One had a moustache and was lean with curly hair.

The other two men were Middle Eastern in appearance. Light brown skin. Both had an air of authority and experience. Lean, fit, and confident. One wore glasses.

The man with glasses had hit him outside with a rifle butt, and the other had shot at him from the porch. The two men looked like brothers, and the leaders—the other two were staring at them deferentially.

All four men were in their mid-to-late twenties, wearing jeans, hiking boots, and green windbreakers over flannel shirts. ISIS usually recruited well-educated single men who were students, either unemployed or with low-paying jobs. ISIS recruits also weren't experts in the Quran. Easier to brainwash.

He had to bury his anger over Blackhood's poor intel about the number of terrorists. The other three must have come in separately.

He glanced around the cabin. The small interior was well-lit by sunshine and had worn pine floors. A door to his right was closed. Bedroom most likely. Next along the back wall was the rear exit door, another open door beyond it—revealing a tiled floor. Probably the bathroom. Then another closed door. Probably a second bedroom.

Steel wondered if the girl was in one of the bedrooms, and if she was still alive. It would be horrible if she was locked up in the same room that held her father's body.

If the girl was still alive, he couldn't imagine the hell she was feeling—that Rachel would feel if he didn't return.

The small kitchen across the room at the south side only had a sink and tiny counter. A small couch and table were in the middle of the room.

He realized the terrorists had shot the old man and woman to lure him and Charlie into a trap. Glancing up again, he focused on the two men who looked like brothers. The one with glasses sat calmly, while his brother had animated hands and a strident voice. Possibly a hothead.

Weapons and spare magazines were piled on the table, including his and Charlie's, along with their communication gear. He caught more words about *making the calls*, but not enough for any new insights.

The man with glasses had a phone on the table plugged into a portable charger. The phone rang, and he answered immediately and listened without talking. He nodded to his associates, speaking three words in Arabic: *It has arrived*. He talked into the phone, but then looked at it, his eyes narrowing. He added *garbage* in Arabic, unplugged the phone charger, and tossed it against a wall.

Abruptly the man rose and walked up to Steel, holding a fixed-blade knife in one hand.

"Let's kill him, Elias," spat the mustached man from the table.

"Not yet." Elias kicked Steel hard in the side.

Steel grunted, his back sliding a few inches along the wall. He had been expecting it.

Elias leaned over and punched him in the face next.

Steel went with the blow, just enough to lessen the impact, but not enough for Elias to notice. Allowing his head to droop against his chest, he gave the impression that he had lost consciousness for a moment. Maybe it would end the attack.

"That's for hurting my friend, Dev." Elias squatted and held up Steel's chin, placing the tip of his knife beneath Steel's right eye. "Do you like the turn of events? You get one chance to avoid more pain." He smiled grimly. "Answer if you understand."

"Sure," he mumbled.

"What's your name?"

"Al."

Elias nodded. "Of course, Al. Our names are real too. It's convenient you carry no ID. Who do you work for?"

Steel decided to keep quiet to see how far they would take things.

"You're American. I can't place what region—and I'm pretty good with dialects. Where are you from, Al?"

Steel didn't reply. His light olive-colored skin was from his mixed heritage of Cajun creole—Spanish, French, Native American, and Caribbean. Impossible to guess. Not that it mattered.

Elias patted Steel's face. "Perhaps you have high pain tolerance." He looked over his shoulder at the mustached man. "Adam."

Adam got up from the table with Steel's silenced Glock in his left hand. He stopped in front of Charlie and pointed the gun at his chest.

Charlie groaned and mumbled, "Don't give them anything."

Adam lifted the Glock a fraction, his trigger finger tightening.

"Wait!" said Steel.

Elias pushed the knife point harder against his cheek. "Who do you work for?"

Steel retreated from the pain, not allowing it to take over his thoughts. "U.S. military."

Elias eased up on the knife. "We already knew that, but it is good to have you verify it. What else do you know?"

Steel wanted confirmation on the terrorists' goal. "Your guide said the three phone contacts were for a major terrorist attack with liquid VX."

"You probably thought he was weak to give you that information, didn't you?" Elias spoke calmly. "Our friend volunteered to go out and perhaps get caught to lure you in."

Steel was glad Elias had confirmed the VX story, but he readjusted his view of the terrorist he had killed. The man had performed his role superbly. "Why risk losing your guide?"

"He was the least committed and thought he could escape." Elias shrugged. "We have a compass, and my brother has an excellent sense of direction. Out of everyone, our guide was the most expendable. Our friend in the boat was our second choice."

Steel believed him. The four in the cabin all appeared dedicated.

Adam stepped closer, pointing the Glock at Steel. "He has nothing we need."

"Patience, Adam." Elias waited calmly until Adam lowered the gun, and then turned back to Steel. "They were foolish to send only three of you."

"Are you sure there's only three of us?" asked Steel.

Elias smirked. "I would have been shot outside if anyone else was in the woods." He cocked his head. "I want to know your extraction process."

"Walking out on our own, just like we came in."

"I don't believe you. You most likely flew into a lake or drove in. You needed some means to cross the river. Which means you're probably leaving the same way. I want to know where and when." He pushed the point of the knife slightly into Steel's cheek.

A drop of blood rolled down Steel's face, but he didn't react. Closing his eyes, he pushed the pain into a compartment where it wouldn't drive him crazy.

If he gave them the correct information, his boat pickup driver would be at risk. Still he began to see a way to keep himself alive a little longer. "I'm traveling south by southwest ten clicks. There's a boat tied up that I can use to cross the river. Then it's another ten clicks to a road and a car."

The pressure of the knife against his face ended. Steel opened his eyes.

"Good job." Elias shrugged and stood up. "Unfortunately we don't have any further need of you. Dev, get the girl. It's time to kill her too."

The big bald man walked to the nearest door, opening it and going inside.

"You need a boat to cross the river." Steel looked up at Elias. "And my boat is hidden."

Elias shrugged. "We'll find our boat or yours. Or we'll swim."

"It's a risk. And the water's frigid."

Elias didn't respond.

Panic. Steel kept it off his face. He could use the OTF knife to cut himself free, but not fast enough before they would shoot him. He could kick Elias, smash his knee, and hurt their leader's ability to move. But he wanted to live. He raced through lies that might make him valuable to them.

In seconds Dev dragged out the girl, holding her wrist.

The first thing Steel recognized was the girl's strength. That surprised him. He had assumed she would be frightened and meek, but her free hand was a fist. However, her lip was trembling and he saw sadness in her eyes—what he would expect to see from Rachel if he didn't return. Small, she had an athletic frame and wore jeans, tennis shoes, and a blue blouse. Her shoulder-length brown hair was in disarray.

The girl bit her lip as she stared at Steel. Maybe ten years old. A bruise had formed on the left side of her face. Someone had slapped her hard.

Seeing the girl's pain reinforced his determination to survive for her. And he couldn't leave his daughter in the same situation either—without a father.

Dev walked the girl over and shoved her to the floor. She flopped down beside Steel, huddling against his side.

Adam raised the Glock.

Steel spoke fast. "I'll take you to my boat. It's not easy to find. You can use it to get into the U.S. A car is waiting on the other side."

"I don't believe you would betray your country so easily." Elias regarded him. "I think you'll lead us into a trap."

"I have a daughter. I want to stay alive." He allowed some desperation into his eyes and voice. "Your plan to get into the U.S. is compromised. If we fail, they plan to capture you at the border. They know your entry point." He didn't think they would buy it, but he wanted to create worry.

The big man at the table spoke in Arabic, and Elias turned to him and responded. The slender man at the table added some comments, also in Arabic.

Steel caught the words *liar* and *kill them*. He was prepared for that.

Elias faced Steel again. "I'm afraid my friends think you are too dangerous." He stepped back, and Adam sneered and aimed the Glock at him.

Steel looked at Elias. "Having a child hostage is to your benefit."

Elias shook his head. "The girl will slow us down."

The solution came to Steel then, and he spoke quickly, his desperation obvious now. "You can zip-tie her to me. I can't run away or fight you if I'm carrying her."

The men all regarded him in silence as he kept talking. "I won't slow you down, and this way you have a child hostage in case you run into any more of my people. And I can guarantee a boat."

Adam hesitated and glanced at Elias.

"Interesting." Elias retreated to the table with Adam, where the four of them whispered in Arabic again.

Finished, Elias walked up to Steel. "All right. You're going with us. But we cannot take your friend in the condition he is in." He looked at Adam.

"Leave him here," said Steel. "He won't be found for weeks. He'll bleed out anyway."

"Too risky." Elias lifted his chin to Adam.

Steel swallowed, unable to think of any other way to save Charlie. He nodded to the girl. "She doesn't have to see this."

"She already witnessed her parents being killed." Elias' eyes held no empathy. "So I doubt it matters."

Before Steel could react, Adam casually stepped forward and shot Charlie twice in the chest—he fell sideways to the floor. The girl buried her face in Steel's shirt.

Steel stared at Charlie, guilt sweeping him. He had lost men on missions in Afghanistan, but to do it here as team leader hit him harder.

"Your turn is coming." Adam pointed the Glock at him. "Both of you."

Steel visualized shooting him in the chest.

CHAPTER 5

ADAM HELD THE GLOCK on Steel, while Dev aimed a P90 at him.

"Stand up and face the wall," ordered Elias.

Steel pulled his knees close to his chest, and then used his hands and legs to slowly push himself up the wall until he was standing. He pivoted on his feet to face the wall, his wrists still bound behind his back.

Elias lifted up the girl, his hands beneath her armpits. "Okay, girl, put your feet through his arms and wrap your arms around his neck."

Steel felt the girl's added weight as she clasped her hands beneath his chin, her legs gripping his waist. She was light. He was thankful for that. His chest ached from the exertions.

Elias used a zip tie to bind the girl's wrists together in front of Steel's neck, and another one to tie her ankles together. Steel wouldn't be able to throw her off, nor brace her weight with his arms. Elias cut his ankle zip tie.

Steel slowly spread his legs and adjusted to the girl's weight. Manageable.

"Dev and Adam, take up the rear," said Elias. "Kaysan and I will lead."

Kaysan was already opening the back door. Oddly, he carried no gun but held Steel's sling bag. Elias strode out after him with Charlie's HK416 and sling bag. Steel followed, passing Adam who carried Steel's Rattler, with a Glock and knife in his belt.

Dev took up the rear, holding a P90 with a Glock stuck in his belt.

Steel noted none of the terrorists were carrying explosives or grenades. They had lied about that too.

As they crossed the grass to the forest, he turned his head slightly and whispered, "What's your name?"

"Lydia," whispered the girl.

"You're very brave, Lydia." He caught her eye. "I'll keep you safe." He wanted to soothe her, but he also needed her to trust him if he wanted any chance to escape.

Elias turned his head as he walked. "Keep talking and I'll shoot both of you."

Steel clamped his lips shut.

They made a weaving line through the first fifty yards of woods. Steel guessed that was to avoid claymores—he actually spotted one covered with leaves.

Lydia's weight forced him to bend forward a little to help keep her centered on his back. She held on tightly with her legs so his arms didn't have to bear her weight. He wondered how long she would be able to keep that up. If her legs tired, she would be forced to cling to his neck with her arms or he would be forced to bend over farther so her weight didn't choke him. He would have to act as soon as possible.

Elias stopped them and held a compass in front of Steel. "Direction to your exit point."

He decided to take them a hundred yards south of his canoe so they wouldn't find it, but close enough if he had to make a run for it. "Directly west by southwest," he said.

Elias regarded him. "Then we'll go southwest."

Steel stared at him steadily. "I'd be a fool to lie."

"And I would be a fool to believe you."

Dev said something in Arabic, and Elias responded.

Steel caught the word *river* and *kill*. They planned to kill him and the girl after they reached the river. Clouds were moving in from the west. Rain could work to his advantage.

Kaysan walked away for a few minutes, returning with Brad's Rattler, Glock, and knife. Then he and Elias strode briskly ahead, everyone moving in single file.

Steel kept up with their quick pace, his mind searching for options. Against four armed men he would have no chance in a fight while he was carrying Lydia. Running with the girl was doable, but even with a diversion the men would gun him down.

He had watched all four men, the way they carried themselves. Kaysan and Elias probably had training in fighting. Dev was strong, but not as dangerous, his movements slower. From what he had seen earlier, Adam looked average in ability.

The only chance he had was to get a gun. That meant he had to have a diversion, cut the zip tie on his wrists, and attack one of the men before the others could react. At first his strategy seemed impossible, but a plan began forming in his mind. It involved elements of movements he had practiced regularly in the virtual reality sims.

He estimated three to four hours to reach the river so he needed to be ready for the right terrain that would give him a high chance of success. He would have only seconds to use the OTF knife, but he had practiced with it repetitively.

Occasionally he spotted chickadees, nuthatches, and squirrels. A few woodpeckers hammered trees in the distance.

The wildlife again reminded him of Rachel and their hikes. It also made him wish he could talk to Lydia, to comfort her and bring some normalcy into the chaos that was now her life. She was quiet, but every now and then he turned his head to catch her eyes and wink at her. After a few times she winked back. He admired her spirit.

The sky clouded over and rain seemed imminent.

He slowed his pace enough to allow Elias and Kaysan to get a little farther ahead, but not enough to spur Dev or Adam to complain as they followed him.

Over and over he visualized exactly what he would do and how it would play out. He used this technique often in Ops to prepare for and optimize success. Combined with endless varying simulations with the virtual reality programs, it gave him confidence and an edge in most situations.

He had practiced what he was about to do with a backpack on his back, but not with someone who could get hurt. His headache had lessened slightly, but it still made it harder to feel sharp.

Raindrops hit his face before he heard them pattering against the ground. It turned into a drizzle, which would disguise some sounds and provide a better excuse for his intended plan.

Behind him, Adam said softly, "Make a run for it, Al. I'll give you a ten-second head start."

Dev swore in Arabic and Adam didn't say anything else.

After an hour of walking Steel began to worry that he wouldn't find the right topography for what he needed. The forest floor was mostly level, with a few small inclines. He would have to give some excuse to Elias to change direction. He tried to think of a reason but came up empty.

And then the ideal terrain appeared.

He paused on the top of a long, steep hill that led down to a narrow gully at the bottom. The small ravine ran north-south as far as he could see. A shorter hill framed the opposite side. Trees covered both hills and were scattered across the narrow bottom.

As he started down he turned slightly sideways, as if he was exercising caution on the wet ground to prevent a fall down the hill. He wanted to make sure Elias and Kaysan crested the opposing hill before he reached the bottom, but he didn't want the two terrorists taking a break at the top to wait for him. Dev and Adam didn't complain about his actions. That gave him some measure of hope.

Elias and Kaysan were striding up the opposing hill at an angle to avoid a massive vertical slab of rock directly opposite him.

Steel moved downhill at the same angle. It would give him a few seconds longer before he reached the bottom. He also wanted to end up south of the two brothers, to block any potential escape by them should he succeed. That might not be possible given they were already south of him. He couldn't afford to wait to see if a better opportunity presented itself.

He also couldn't prepare Lydia for what was going to happen. But if she cried out it would bring Elias and Kaysan back fast. The only solution was to risk telling her. He did it while stepping on a branch to make some noise, his head turned downhill away from Adam and Dev.

"Don't cry out when I fall," he whispered. "Close your eyes."

Her eyes widened, but she blinked back at him and then closed her eyes, gripping him firmly. She understood. She might end up badly injured, but he couldn't help it. They were both going to die if he couldn't escape. Thus he disregarded any concerns for her and focused.

Kaysan had already disappeared over the crest of the opposing hill. Elias was at the top, moving steadily. Steel prayed the man kept going.

Two-thirds of the way down the hill, he glanced up again. Elias was no longer visible. Making sure he had a decent stretch below him that was clear of trees, he pretended to catch his right, downhill foot on something. Teetering, he fell down onto his right side, creating some momentum by deliberately rolling.

Lydia gripped him tightly as he rolled down the rest of the hill, faster and faster. He hoped the speed made it easier on Lydia who had to bear his weight momentarily during each revolution.

Near the bottom he slammed into a tree with his shoulder and chest. He grunted.

He had ended up on his left side so he immediately rolled to his right side to hide his back from Adam and Dev. The two men were a dozen strides behind him. He didn't know if Elias was watching from the hill behind him.

Now or never.

He pulled up the back of his shirt, grabbed the OTF knife from its sheath, and cut his zip tie in a few quick motions.

Lydia was quiet. Either stunned, unconscious, or just acting.

Keeping his arms behind his back, he worked to get to his knees, still facing the men. Adam held the Rattler in his left hand, the carry strap looped over his head, Dev held the P90 in his right hand.

Steel hoped Adam would grab one of his arms to help him up. He made sure the knife was out of sight. Dev reached the bottom a few yards north of Adam, pausing there.

"Idiot." Adam stopped near Steel's head.

Dev spoke sharply to Adam again.

For a moment Steel thought Adam wouldn't help him up or would kick him. He prepared himself.

But Adam let the Rattler hang on its strap as he leaned over and gripped Steel beneath his left armpit with both hands.

Steel allowed Adam to help lift him until he had his right foot firmly planted on the ground. Then he pushed up. Grabbing Adam's left arm with his left hand while rising, he jabbed the knife. Adam's right arm blocked his heart, thus he aimed low, scoring the lower part of Adam's arm and plunging the knife into his stomach.

Adam's mouth opened, his eyes wide. He slumped against Steel.

Dev stepped forward, raising the P90.

Steel shoved Adam's head down with his left hand, twisted toward Dev, and slashed his left carotid. Dev gaped, firing the P90 wide as he staggered back several steps and fell.

Using his left hand, Steel reached for the Glock in Adam's belt, but the man had somehow pulled his knife and jabbed at him.

Steel tried to twist away, but Lydia's weight slowed him. A searing pain erupted in his left side.

Adam pushed himself away, falling to his side and fumbling with the Glock with his left hand.

"Dev! Adam!"

Elias.

Steel's actions were frenzied. He kicked Adam in the groin and the man convulsed over onto the Glock, groaning. Steel ripped the Rattler carry strap off Adam's head, and then straddled the man, pushing him over to his back. He grabbed the Glock with his left hand, the Rattler with his right—while still holding the knife.

Adam feebly grabbed the Glock, and Steel squeezed the trigger, shooting him in the chest. The man released the gun and collapsed.

"Dev! Adam!" Elias was closer.

Kaysan would try to box him in from the south.

Steel bolted.

CHAPTER 6

STEEL SPRINTED SOUTH ALONG the gully, his side on fire.
Through it all, Lydia had remained quiet. Maybe she had
been injured in the fall. But she still gripped him tightly
with her legs and arms. He glanced over his right shoulder at
the hill.

Elias was aiming the assault rifle at him.

Steel lurched behind a tree as shots were fired. Elias called to
his brother.

Steel shoved the Glock into his belt, dropped the Rattler, and
cut Lydia's ankle and wrist zip ties. Quickly he lowered her to
the ground, gently pushing her back against the tree trunk. Rain
dripped down her face and her eyes were still squeezed shut.

He sheathed the OTF knife, slung the Rattler carry strap over
his head, and peered around the tree.

Elias was working his way down the hill north of him, the
HK416 aimed in their direction. Steel didn't have a clear shot
past the trees between them. He fired a burst from the Rattler
to slow the man down and make him think twice about rushing
him.

Elias disappeared behind a tree.

Steel glanced at Lydia. Her eyes were open and she stared up
at him.

Colonel Danker's words flashed through him; *civilians are
expendable, too much is at stake, the mission comes first.* But there
was nowhere Lydia could run to for safety. If he left her, Elias
would shoot her within a minute. Worse, Elias might torture her
to try to get him to give himself up. Which he wouldn't do.

Without Lydia he would be a corpse in the cabin now. Rachel's image flashed through him. No choice.

He wrapped an arm around her waist, lifted her up, and backed away, keeping the tree between him and Elias. "Hang on," he murmured.

She wrapped her legs around his waist, her arms around his neck, pressing the side of her head against his shoulder.

He couldn't afford to let the two brothers get him in a crossfire in the bottom of the gully.

Another bullet from Elias bit the ground to the right of his feet. He moved slightly left, to see past the tree. Elias was running down the hill. Steel fired another burst from the Rattler, forcing the terrorist to stop again for cover.

Immediately he turned and ran west, straight up the hill. They wouldn't expect it.

A shot chipped the bark of a tree trunk inches from his face. He paused behind it and fired a longer burst in Elias' direction.

Carrying both guns, he kept going, past more trees that partially hid him. His goal was to get to the top of the hill north of Kaysan, and hopefully have Elias below him.

A bullet chewed the dirt ahead of him.

Then Elias was yelling to his brother—Steel guessed to tell him to return north.

He leaned forward, knowing one false step could send him slipping into a fall. Even though Lydia was light, he was starting to tire with her weight. A survival run.

He could hear Danker in his mind again, telling him to dump the girl. He couldn't do it. He would want someone to save Rachel in this situation. His conditioning and adrenaline allowed him to keep going.

At the top of the hill he stopped behind a big red pine, breathing hard, his side aching. He didn't see any good hiding places so the tree would have to do. He lowered Lydia to the ground.

"Sit down," he whispered, squatting. "Keep your back against the tree and don't move."

She obeyed, staring up at him, her lips trembling.

He straightened and stepped slightly to the right of the tree trunk. Elias was running between trees in the gully, making himself a difficult target. Steel fired a longer burst from the Rattler, but Elias dove behind a log.

Steel let the Rattler hang from the strap and fired several shots from the Glock into the log. He wanted to give Elias second thoughts about moving anytime soon.

He pulled up his shirt to look at his side. The cut bled and probably needed stitches.

Squatting beside Lydia, he whispered, "Don't move. No noise. Can you do that?"

She crossed her arms as if hugging herself and nodded.

"My name is Jack and I'm coming back for you."

She looked up at him, a forlorn look in her eyes.

Steel swore to himself that he wouldn't fail her. "I promise."

He ran away from her, west, looking for any sign of Kaysan along the hilltop to the south. Danker's voice echoed in his ears again; *You're jeopardizing the whole mission because of one girl whose life doesn't matter—you're being weak*. He ignored those thoughts.

Elias called out in Arabic to Kaysan.

Steel heard enough to understand Elias was giving his brother his position. He had to kill one of the brothers now while they were separated. Elias would be wary of coming up the hill now, not knowing where he was.

He ran farther west. After fifty yards he glimpsed a figure to the southeast. Carefully he circled back from tree to tree, wanting to come up behind Kaysan from the south. If Elias or Kaysan found Lydia they would hurt her and he didn't want to be a spectator to her torture.

He advanced slowly, making sure he didn't step on broken branches and give away his position. He would never be able to approach Kaysan then. From behind a tree he slid to one side, peeking out.

Kaysan had stopped behind a large boulder, fifty feet south of Lydia and just as far from the top of the hill. Steel couldn't see him.

Kaysan called out to his brother.

Steel heard the words for *girl* and *trap*. Kaysan assumed Lydia was a trap to lure them out into the open. That would make both brothers cautious about advancing and worked to his advantage.

He ran southeast, fifty feet south of the boulder. Just past the rock Kaysan's back came into view. Steel stopped behind a tree, raising the Rattler.

Kaysan whirled around, firing.

Steel threw himself to the ground on his belly and elbows, firing his gun. Kaysan also cast himself to the ground, firing at the same time. They both missed.

Steel rolled behind a tree, while Kaysan scrambled behind the front of the boulder.

Kaysan called to Elias again.

Elias would come up the hill fast now. Steel put a bullet into the edge of the boulder to keep Kaysan behind it. Rising, he ran forward northeast. Stopping behind a tree, he picked up a stick and threw it high and west of Kaysan's position, far past the other side of the rock.

Immediately he walked out from behind the tree, striding toward Kaysan's hiding place, the Rattler stock in his shoulder.

The stick hit the ground.

Kaysan shifted his position to the east side of the rock, crouching and partially in view. Steel fired a burst, hitting him in the shoulder.

Kaysan slumped to his knees and turned, trying to raise his weapon.

Steel emptied the magazine into him, sending the terrorist sprawling to his back.

Elias called out his brother's name.

Steel ran to the dead man. He searched the body, finding a spare mag for the Rattler—which he loaded into his gun. He also found a compass and phone. He ejected the partially spent magazine in Kaysan's Rattler and pocketed it. Thinking ahead, he decided to take Kaysan's Glock.

He quickly went prone and crawled toward the edge of the hill.

Elias was halfway up the slope, running toward Lydia. Taking aim, Steel fired his Glock three times, but Elias threw himself to the ground out of sight. Steel might have hit him—he wasn't sure. The man was careful and experienced. Maybe ex-military.

Feeling more in control of the situation, Steel decided to wait him out for the moment. He had a clear view of the gully and the upper part of the hill.

To the north, Lydia still sat against the tree, watching him. He motioned her to run west. She scrambled to her feet and ran.

Relieved, he surveyed the gully, debating on what to do next. He glanced west to track Lydia.

She was running hard but stopped abruptly. She didn't move again or make a sound.

He didn't understand why. He looked carefully. Not far ahead of her the two bear cubs he had spotted on his arrival were sniffing the ground. The mother wouldn't be far behind.

CHAPTER 7

AT FIRST STEEL COULDN'T understand why the mother bear didn't sense Lydia's presence.

A slight breeze was blowing from the west so the bear must not have picked up her scent. The continuing drizzle probably helped too. The adult bear was probably on the opposite side of the tree.

If he went south or north the cubs would see him. Then the mother might circle the tree and see Lydia. Ditto if he went to her. He didn't move.

Lydia backed up. One step at a time.

Steel caught glimpses of the cubs moving through the forest, but the mother was still hidden. Lydia reached a large pine. Once she was behind it she pressed her back to it and stopped. Her eyes wide, she stared at Steel.

He held up a palm for her to stay and pressed a finger to his lips. She didn't need the last reminder, but he gave it anyway. He glanced down the hill again. No sign of Elias.

The cubs changed course, heading in Lydia's direction. Sniffing the ground, they were probably looking for food. Horrified, he hurriedly waved her toward him. After taking another quick look at the gully, he rose and sprinted toward her.

Lydia ran flat out, her face white and her gait stiff. What amazed him was her ability to remain quiet in the face of danger.

Elias called out Kaysan's name again.

Steel wondered what the man would do when he figured out his brother was dead.

Lydia was thirty feet from him, still running hard, when a black blur bolted around the tree behind her. Immediately Steel stopped and raised the Rattler.

The charging mother bear was directly behind Lydia. He didn't have a shot. He strode forward, firing into the air until the ammo ran out. He loaded the last mag.

The bear slid to a stop, its ears pinned back, and slapped the ground with a paw.

To minimize any sense of aggression, Steel stared at the animal's feet, not its eyes. He knew enough to interpret the bear's behavior as nervous and apprehensive, but not really interested in attacking.

Lydia ran until she wrapped her arms around his waist, sliding behind him. Tense, Steel didn't move.

The bear lifted its nose to sniff the air, yawned, and then turned to rejoin her cubs.

Taking a deep breath, Steel pulled Lydia behind a tree. Sobbing, her shoulders shaking, Lydia gripped him tightly. It was probably the first time since her parents and grandfather had died that she had let her emotions loose. He couldn't imagine what her losses would do to her life.

"You're safe now, Lydia," he said quietly. "I won't let anyone hurt you again."

She kept crying.

He kept a hand on her shoulder, while scanning for Elias. The terrorist wasn't visible. It worried him. Elias might be making a run for his primary exit. The VX nerve agent might be taking precedence over concerns for his brother.

The thought of VX nerve agent ending up in U.S. water supplies set his teeth on edge. He had jeopardized the mission by taking care of Lydia. Without her, he would have approached things differently. Without her he would also be dead.

His hope was that Elias was injured, but he couldn't wait any longer to find out. Kneeling, he held Lydia by her arms.

She looked at him, sniffling.

He hated what he had to say. "I need you to be brave one more time."

She was quiet, but he saw fear in her eyes.

"I'll take you to a safer place, but then I have to leave you for a while. We have to go now." Unwilling to wait any longer, he stood, wincing at the thought of Rachel in this position. "When I wave, you run after me as fast as you can. Just follow me. Run from tree to tree but stay a good distance behind me. Alright?"

She nodded.

"Good." He peered through the drizzle. Not seeing anything of concern, he said, "Come on."

He hurried back to Kaysan and took the sling bag off him. He handed the bag to Lydia, held up a hand for her to stay put, and ran south along the top of the hill. All the while he inspected the gully below. No sign of Elias.

He waved to Lydia to follow, while continuing along the top of the hill. At the gully's southern end, he ran a zigzag path down the hill, using trees for cover while watching for Elias. No shots. It gave him a sinking feeling.

If Elias had left, the man would have a decent head start on him. Chasing him with his side injury wouldn't be easy. The light rain was also beginning to chill him. Still he trained hard at home and ran often. He hoped Elias wasn't a conditioned athlete.

He waved Lydia to follow him, and ran down to the bottom, and then south. After fifty feet he noted a footprint, also pointed south. A hundred yards later the gully ended in a long, gently sloping hill.

He waved to Lydia again, and then bolted up the hill, using trees as much as possible to hide his ascent. If Elias was going to ambush him, this was the perfect place. Silence.

At the top of the hill he saw two things to his liking: a shoeprint leading southeast, which fit for an exit strategy for Elias, and a large pine tree with a wide cleft in its bottom. He waited impatiently for Lydia to run up the hill.

When she joined him, he pointed to the recess in the tree trunk. "Sit in there, facing out, and point the gun out. If the bear or anything else comes at you, fire the gun until you kill it." He unscrewed the silencer from the Glock he'd taken off Kaysan. "It will make more noise this way."

She stared at the opening in the tree trunk.

He knew she didn't want to go in. "I have to go now. There's food and a compass in the sling bag. Do you know how to use a compass, Lydia?"

She nodded. "My grandpa showed me."

"Good. If I don't return by dark, use the compass to go west to the river. Then go north along the river until you find a canoe to cross it. Then keep going west." An adult wouldn't want to hear all of that and he hated saying it to a ten-year-old girl. "Repeat it to me."

"West to the river. Follow the river north. Then take the canoe across and go west." She looked at him, and then climbed into the trunk and sat down.

Clicking the safety off, he moved to the side of her and handed her the gun. "Hold it between your legs."

She wrapped her hands around the grip. Setting the gun against her waist, the barrel facing out between her legs, she squeezed her knees together to prop it up. Carefully she put a finger around the trigger.

"If the bear comes, just stay here. Don't make any sounds. If it attacks just keep pulling the trigger." He couldn't imagine leaving Rachel in this situation. "I'm coming back. I promise. Okay?"

Biting her lip, she gave a small nod.

He had to let go of any concerns for her so he could focus. He whirled and ran.

CHAPTER 8

TRAVELING IN THE DIRECTION of the last print he had discovered, Steel ran southeast at a good clip, switching the Rattler from hand to hand.

The rain ended, but the ground was still wet and slippery. He was glad he had boots. His headache had eased a little, but he was tired. The knife wound added to his fatigue and his ears were still ringing.

While he ran he looked for footprints or any other signs of Elias. After ten minutes he didn't see anything so he ran a weaving pattern, back and forth. It slowed his forward progress but gave him a better chance to spot tracks. He ignored the pain in his side.

After twenty minutes without seeing anything, he widened his pattern. He almost cheered when a broken branch appeared on the ground with a partial print. Judging direction from the angle of the print, he headed directly south.

To be safe he slowed to a fast walk while looking for a second print to verify he was going in the right direction. He found it, and then decided to run hard in a straight line, using the compass to stay on track. The cloudy sky hid the sun and any possible bearing.

After another thirty minutes of hard running he came to a small creek. Scattered patches of sand were on both sides. He looked for tracks again on the near side first, running along it thirty yards in either direction. Nothing.

He splashed across the ankle-deep water and inspected the opposite side. He was rewarded with a print farther south, and followed it slowly to the next, where it turned into the woods. There he spotted another. He ran hard again.

Looking ahead, he scoured the forest for glimpses of Elias' green flannel shirt or any sign of movement. He started to worry that the man was too far ahead of him.

Thirty minutes later, his side burning, he stopped. A faint noise. He cocked his head to listen, trying to filter past the ringing in his ears. Another faint sound. Straight ahead. He sprinted.

Ahead of him a stand of birch trees broke up the pine, enabling him to have a farther line of sight. A flash of green flannel appeared a hundred yards in the distance. Exhilarated, he corrected his direction to intercept the terrorist.

He was running so hard he almost missed spotting Elias aiming the HK416 at him from beside a tree. He jumped sideways as Elias fired a burst. Not waiting, he bolted right, still moving fast, using trees for protection.

Unless Elias was a trained marksman, he would have a difficult time hitting him on the run where there was cover.

Three shots.

Steel's upper left arm abruptly burned. He gasped and almost fell down, stumbling several steps before he steadied himself. Glancing at his arm, he saw a bloody furrow across the back of the triceps.

Ducking, he ran faster, noting Elias' position while weaving and making himself a harder target to hit.

More rifle reports.

Steel scurried among the trees, glancing east. Elias ran from his position. Changing direction, Steel sprinted in direct pursuit again.

In three minutes he saw the terrorist fifty yards ahead of him running through the trees. He wanted the man alive but couldn't risk letting him escape. He fired a burst from the Rattler. Missed.

Elias whirled, stopped, and fired a burst from the hip.

Steel dodged to the right, didn't slow down, and closed the distance. Elias aimed at him again. Nothing. Empty magazine. Steel ran right at him, the Rattler raised in his right hand.

Elias turned and ran.

Aiming at Elias' legs, Steel pulled the trigger. Empty. He had wasted bullets on scaring the bear to protect Lydia. Another unnecessary risk. He let the Rattler hang, pulled the Glock, and fired three shots at Elias' fading back. Too many trees.

Shifting the Rattler to his back, he pumped his legs. He noted with concern that Elias had a smooth stride. The man was a runner. Under normal conditions Steel could wear him down, but injured and tired he didn't know if he could catch him.

Stopping, he took careful aim and fired several shots. Too much foliage. Elias had crouched low, veered left, and kept going. Worried he couldn't catch him, Steel fired two more quick shots.

Elias kept going.

Running a short sprint, Steel stopped again and fired several times. Thick forest blocked his shots. But then Elias burst into view. Steel pressed the trigger. Empty. Swearing, he dropped the gun and ran.

The idea of failing and allowing VX to threaten millions didn't allow him to slow his gait. His lungs burned.

Within minutes he was gaining. Elias was tiring too. Thirty yards separated them. Elias glanced back, and then spurted ahead. Steel couldn't match his stride, but soon Elias slowed down again.

Steel ignored his heaving lungs and drained legs. Desperate, he blocked out everything except keeping his legs moving in a smooth rhythm, focusing on Elias' back.

Elias slowed more.

Steel wove around a tree, relieved to see he was only ten yards behind him now. The terrorist slowed even more, but Steel could also feel the toll on his body. It was now or never. One last effort. He burst forward.

In seconds he pushed Elias from behind and sent him tumbling.

Instead of crumpling, Elias rolled smoothly over the ground and rose to his feet fluidly, ending up in a martial arts stance, his open hands raised and ready.

Steel stopped abruptly. He unslung and dropped the Rattler and drew the OTF knife. His lungs heaved and his body felt drained. While running through scenarios in his mind, he needed a delay to recover.

"You don't have to do this, Elias," he gasped. "You can choose to walk away." He walked toward Elias, who was also breathing hard. The man's glasses were askew on his face, but his eyes betrayed no fear.

"Was Kaysan your brother?" Steel wanted him off-balance. "He didn't put up much of a fight before he died."

Elias said matter-of-factly, "We were both prepared to die. I accept his death." His eyes glinted. "After I kill you, I'm going back to finish the girl."

Steel believed him. A moment of rage filled his head but he immediately squelched it. Stepping to the side, he swung his knife at Elias' arm. Elias blocked the strike, while turning into him, elbowing Steel in the stomach while simultaneously grabbing his knife arm.

Steel was ready for the stomach blow and twisted out of his grip. Elias threw a kick. Steel turned sideways to avoid it, dropped to a knee, and scored Elias' calf with the knife.

Gasping, Elias aimed a series of strikes at Steel's head.

From his knees Steel rolled away. Before he could rise Elias rushed forward and kicked him in the ribs. Steel rolled again, numb with pain, and ended up prone on his stomach. Maybe a broken rib. For a moment he couldn't move. If he didn't end this quickly he might end up dead.

He lay motionless on the ground, groaning, his eyes barely open. Another scenario he had practiced repeatedly in the VR sims.

Elias took two steps toward him, raising a foot to stomp his head.

Twisting to his side, Steel cut the Achilles tendon of the foot Elias stood on. Screaming, Elias fell on top of him. Steel gasped in pain.

Trying to turn over onto his back, Steel raised an arm to block Elias' fists. One blow connected with the side of his head, stunning him for a moment. Gathering himself, he had to let go of the knife to push against the soil, twisting violently to his back. He drove his folded knuckles into the front of Elias' neck.

Elias gasped, pulled back, and managed to hit him in the chest and torso, and then his ribs again.

Steel almost blacked out from the pain, but his survival instincts took over. He palmed Elias in the lower ribs. The man gasped and fell off him to his back, choking for air. Steel thought he might have pushed one of Elias' floating ribs into a lung.

Rolling away, it took several gasping breaths before he could slowly push to his knees, and then his feet. It felt like he'd been run over. Breathing was painful and he hurt everywhere. Definitely a cracked or broken rib.

Elias wasn't moving and wheezed deeply, remaining on his back, staring up at the sky. The man had lost his glasses.

Stumbling over to him, Steel noted the terrorist still had the sling bag. He kicked Elias in the head and the terrorist went limp.

It took him a minute to use zip ties from the sling bag to bind Elias' wrists, ankles, and ankles to wrists. Each time he moved he winced, but he kept his breathing shallow so he didn't expand his diaphragm.

Finished, he sat a few feet away, the sling bag on his lap, his back against a tree trunk. Feeling weak, he peeked at his side wound. A bruise surrounded his ribs and the cut was still bleeding. His upper arm was also bloody. He searched the sling bag for the first-aid kit.

After applying antiseptic, he taped four-by-four gauze over his wounds. It stopped the bleeding. He quickly searched the sling bag and Elias' pockets, but the man's phone was gone. Elias must have considered it a risk and tossed it at some point during his flight. Not worth searching for it. He already had the numbers, and Kaysan's phone.

When Elias came to, the terrorist looked at him calmly, wincing as he wheezed for air.

Steel toyed with the knife in his hands. "Do you like the turn of events? You get one chance to avoid pain." He smiled grimly. "Answer if you understand."

"Go to hell," Elias wheezed.

Steel slowly stood up, hobbled over, and kicked him in the side. Elias groaned, his face strained.

"Where are the VX barrels?"

"You'll never find them," gasped Elias. "And they'll send someone else to deliver them. You've failed no matter what you do to me."

Steel thought about that. If Elias could withstand pain, he might not get any more information. He stared at the terrorist.

An idea came to him. "The girl almost got mauled by a bear. I think if you can't tell me what I need to know, I add more zip ties and you wait to see what comes along that's hungry. Wolverines love to scavenge on carcasses too."

Elias stared at him, hate in his eyes.

Steel spoke softly. "Your friends are all dead. It's just you now. Why not live to fight another day?"

His breathing still shallow, Elias didn't answer.

"Three phone numbers were on Kaysan's phone for three VX barrels. I memorized the numbers." He pulled out more zip ties from the sling bag. Kneeling, he added them to Elias' wrists and ankles, ensuring the man would have no chance to escape.

Finished, Steel looped the bag over his head and positioned it on his back. Painfully he rose to his feet. "Last chance. Tell me how to find the barrels and I'll let you go. Otherwise you stay here—food for passersby. Something is going to smell your blood."

Elias looked up at him, his voice hoarse. "You're why your country needs to suffer."

"Give me something. You can't help ISIS by letting a bear have you for dinner."

Elias didn't speak.

Steel turned and walked away, recovering the Rattler and slinging it over his head so it rested against his back too.

Elias whispered, "You're right. The phone numbers are the contacts for the barrels."

Steel stopped to face him. "I already know that."

"You call, give a password, and they give you directions to the barrels."

"Why don't the contacts just take care of the barrels themselves?"

"They have families and jobs." Elias lifted his chin. "They blend in. They can be used again for other actions."

That made sense to him. And he didn't detect any signs that Elias was lying. "What's the password?"

"Take these zip ties off me first." Elias looked up at him, his breathing still labored.

"We'll just track down the numbers and the contacts, and someone more skilled than myself will talk to them." Steel leaned over. "My guess is that if your contacts have jobs and families, they won't be as tough as you and have a lot more to lose and more reasons to bargain." He straightened. "Either way, I can't trust any password you give me."

"Without the passwords you have nothing."

"I have the phone numbers." He put the sling bag on his back and walked away.

"Wait," whispered Elias. "I'll tell you."

Steel paused, regarding Elias.

Elias said, "For the first phone number the password is the Arabic word for twenty-five—the number of prophets named in the Quran. The second is the Arabic word for seven, the number of sins that doom a person to hell, and the third is the Arabic word for ninety-nine—the number of names of Allah."

Steel stared at the man. It sounded plausible. But Elias had advanced training and could be skilled in lying, possibly giving him false passwords or in the wrong order to warn the three contacts. The higher-ups could sort it out. "Thanks, Elias."

There was a small chance Elias would be found by a hiker or the Canadian police before he died, and then get access to a phone and warn ISIS about the leak for the VX barrel locations. He was still a risk.

Elias wheezed. "You gave me your word."

Steel spoke softly. "You killed a little girl's parents and grandfather in front of her. You killed my two operatives. You're a murderer and your only purpose in life is to continue murdering."

"You're a liar."

"I can live with that." Steel considered his options. The OTF knife, zip ties around the neck, or his hands. None of it felt appealing.

When he finished killing Elias, he walked away, never looking back.

CHAPTER 9

STEEL RECOVERED HIS GLOCK and the HK416, slinging the latter over a shoulder, the pistol shoved under his belt. Unable to signal Lydia with the gun, he hoped she had remained where he left her.

He used the compass to backtrack. It was slow going. Pain assaulted him on every step and with every breath. Pacing himself, he kept the pain in the background, while following his tracks along the way he had come. The terrain didn't seem familiar because he'd been running hard through it before.

When he reached the stream, he stood in the middle and cupped his hands, dipping them in to drink some water. If he had to take parasite drugs later, that was better than passing out on the trail due to dehydration. He took the canteen out of the bag and filled it, returning it to the bag.

As he walked he felt lucky to be alive. His training had paid off. Still the mission was only half-completed. He had to get the phone numbers to Colonel Danker.

What he really wanted now was to return to Rachel and Carol. His thoughts continually turned to them. He couldn't wait to see them, to hold them in his arms. He missed them terribly. Considering how close he had come to losing them, and causing them grief, he realized how lucky he was.

He would quit Blackhood Ops, go caving with Rachel, and take her and Carol to a cabin. Enjoy life with his loved ones. It seemed so simple he wondered why it had taken him so long to see it.

Nearly three hours later he recognized the hill at the south end of the gully, and the tree Lydia had been hiding in. From fifty feet away he still couldn't see her, since the trunk opening faced north. It couldn't be more than mid-afternoon, but the clouds were turning the forest darker. At least they had plenty of time to make the rendezvous point before midnight.

"Lydia!" *Please be there.* He didn't want to believe all his efforts to keep her alive had been for nothing.

After another half-dozen steps, he stopped. Soft sounds to his right. A large pine tree had broken near the base and fallen, and the trunk formed a narrow angle to the ground. Branches and leaves made it hard to see what was behind it. Maybe Lydia had moved there for safety.

"Lydia?" he said quietly. She might be hurt. He stepped forward to see behind the log, but froze almost immediately. Black fur was visible just above the trunk. He slowly drew the OTF knife. Near the end of the log a bear cub appeared, sniffing along the ground. It paused to look up at him.

One moment he was watching it, the next he was sliding over the ground in a confusion of limbs. He came to a stop and painfully rolled over to his back. A black bear loomed over him, straddling his legs. He had lost the OTF knife and swept his hand over the ground to find it.

Shots were fired, sounding close.

The bear swung its head north, and then stood up on two feet.

Steel rolled his head to the side. Lydia was walking toward him, the Glock held in both hands and aimed at the bear. Her bravery astounded him. He wanted to tell her to run.

Instead she stopped and fired the gun again. The bear dropped to all fours, spun, and ran off, the cubs in tow.

"Good girl," he murmured. It was then that he felt the pain—a sharp stinging across his upper back. It felt like the bear had torn him open. His body was limp. Used up. He wondered if he was dying. He realized the Rattler and rifle had been torn off his body.

Lydia knelt beside him, setting the Glock down.

"Just give me a minute," he gasped. He stared up at her. "Are you okay?"

She nodded. "Did you catch the bad man?"

"He won't hurt anyone. We're safe now." He wanted to change the topic. "Can you see if there's anything on the ground by my feet? I think the bear might have torn my sling bag."

She crawled away for a minute, returning with a handful of items, including beef jerky, protein bars, and a small flashlight.

"Why don't you open two of those bars and we'll have some lunch." He wanted to smile but his back burned now.

She complied and they chewed in silence.

An owl gave a *po-po-po-po* whistle in the distance.

He grimaced over the pain everywhere on his body. He didn't want to move. He couldn't. "What kind of owl do you think it is, Lydia?" he whispered.

She listened. "I don't know."

"Boreal owl. I have a daughter your age who loves birds. We have contests on hikes to see who can name the most species."

Her eyes glistened.

He took a deep breath. "I'm hurt, Lydia. I need to rest. Can you sit by me and watch out for the bear?"

"Okay." She sat and crossed her legs.

"I won't sleep too long," he whispered. He was out immediately.

Sometime later, he wasn't sure when, something pricked his attention, pulling him out of a dark, restful place he didn't want to leave. He cracked his eyes open. His vision was blurry from sleep and welcoming dreams. Not far away he saw legs. Someone standing. A rescue party? His gaze moved upward.

A man was hunched over, clutching his chest with one hand, a knife gripped in his other.

Adam.

CHAPTER 10

S TEEL'S FIRST THOUGHT WAS how the hell had the man survived this long? He guessed Adam could ask that of him too.

Lydia was standing, holding the Glock with both hands and aiming it at the terrorist.

Steel wanted to tell her to pull the trigger, but his lips and throat seemed too dry to get the words out.

Adam lurched forward, raising the knife.

Two explosions. Lydia's Glock.

Before he closed his eyes, Steel saw Adam falling.

Sometime later his shoulder rocked back and forth until he opened his eyes again. Rachel was beside him. It surprised him and he wanted to hold her, but his arms wouldn't move.

"Rachel," he murmured.

"C'mon," she said.

"I can't," he mumbled. A tear escaped his eye. He was failing his daughter. "I'm sorry, Rachel."

"Lydia!"

He blinked. Lydia stared down at him. The confusion of the dream slipped away.

The forest was darker. Panic. For a moment he thought they had missed the midnight pickup. His voice was hoarse. "Walk to the pickup point. Get help, Lydia. Then we can go home."

She just stared at him.

He realized why. She had no home. It was an effort just to move his lips. "Do you have any aunts or uncles?"

"Aunt Mary. She's my mom's twin sister."

"That's great. Where does she live?"

"Michigan."

"Do you like her?" he murmured.

She nodded.

He closed his eyes, unable to hold off his fatigue anymore.

"Jack!"

He blinked. Lydia was shaking his shoulder again. Blood loss made him weak. "I can't walk on my own."

"I'll help you." She looked down at him, a determined expression on her face.

Maybe he could cover a little distance. Get her started. He dreaded the pain that would bring. "All right," he whispered. "Let's get out of here so you can see your aunt."

With her help he slowly eased himself onto his side, and then sat up, gasping. Tears filled his eyes. Shifting to his knees, he reached out to Lydia. She grasped his arm and helped him to his feet. He staggered under the burning sensation that shot across his back. Bending over, he groaned.

Lydia handed him the Glock and he feebly stuck it in his belt. They would have to leave the other guns.

"Find my knife."

She did, and he had her place it in the belt-sheath for him.

"Flashlight," he gasped. "You hold it."

She picked it up. Taking a breath, he wrapped an arm around her shoulders and leaned on her for support. He didn't want to move. Every movement either burned his back or stabbed his ribs. Using the compass, he set a course for northwest.

He paused to stare at Adam. Face down. He looked at Lydia.

"I shot him." She stared at the body.

Her voice was steady and that gave him hope her action wouldn't traumatize her further.

"You did the right thing. You were protecting me and yourself. You're very brave." Amazed again at her strength, he squeezed her shoulder.

She looked up at him, her face strained, her voice wavering. "I didn't shoot the bear because I didn't want the cubs to lose their mother."

Like you lost your mother. "Your mother would be proud of you. I am too." For a moment he felt horrible that he hadn't saved her mother, and that Lydia wouldn't have a mother to love her all her life. He had to get her to her aunt. It gave him strength and determination to stay upright at least until they reached the canoe.

She wiped her eyes and he shuffled forward. It was slow going. He had to steel himself to the fact that they had miles to go. Heading northwest, they passed Kaysan.

Steel stopped to lean against a tree. He closed his eyes, half-awake.

In seconds Lydia was nudging him. "Come on."

For a moment he wavered, and then she tugged him forward. He leaned on her shoulder with his hand.

The pain came at him in waves and often he had to stop. Every step hurt. Lydia kept him from falling. He wasn't going to make it.

The canoe, he told himself. For Lydia. For Rachel.

He paced himself, leaning on her the whole time. After a while he could sense her tiring beneath his weight, but he couldn't remain upright on his own. His back felt wet where the bear had struck him. He tried to ignore it.

During the walk he kept his eyes barely cracked open, enough to see his feet. A deep sense of satisfaction swept him that he had saved Lydia. It would help her that she had saved him from the bear and Adam—and was saving him now. Anything to give her strength to face her losses was good.

It made him realize again how strong the girl was, and how strong Rachel was—he should have climbed the vertical chute cave with her. They had found it on one of their adventures. She had wanted to do it, but he had told her she wasn't ready. She was. He was the one who hadn't been ready—always obsessed with the nth degree of safety.

Rachel needed to know he believed in her, trusted her. He should have let her do easy caves by herself to gain confidence. He could have monitored her while allowing her to go in alone. Imagining her face lighting up when he told her his decision gave him strength to fight the pain and motivation to keep shuffling forward.

They stopped frequently so they could both rest. A number of times he mumbled, "You're very brave, Lydia. Thank you."

It took the better part of four hours to reach the river and find the canoe. Lydia pushed it into the water, wrapping the canoe line around a log. Steel just stared at it, exhausted.

Lydia returned to the tree he was leaning against. He didn't want to move.

"Come on." She moved closer to him.

Just across the river. Then he could tell her to go on her own. He carefully put his arm across her shoulders.

"Okay," he murmured. He stumbled down to the canoe, collapsing into it, and managed to get himself onto a seat to paddle. That effort made him gasp.

He let Lydia do most of the work, while he remained bent over, trying to guide the canoe from the stern. The sky cleared, showing an early moon. For a moment they stopped to look at it, while they drifted on the river. It was all he could do to keep from passing out.

After the crossing, Lydia got out and pulled the canoe a few feet onto the sand. He stared at the water, not wanting to get out. She splashed into the water by the canoe and reached for him.

He grabbed her hands and stood up, wobbly. When he stepped out of the canoe, his toe on caught on the gunwale and he fell face first into the river. Water surrounded him and he gulped it down. He reached out to push off the bottom but couldn't feel it. Panicked, he tried to stand, but couldn't orient his feet.

Lydia's arm slipped beneath his shoulder and he used her to brace his feet in the mud. He worked himself upright, coughing water and gasping. The water was cold, actually a balm for his back.

He stood hunched over, hacking to get water out of his lungs. After a minute he trudged through the mud to the shore with Lydia pressed against his leg and side, helping him stay upright.

Once out of the water, he paused and closed his eyes—and almost fell over.

"Keep walking, Jack!"

He opened his eyes and obeyed, not stopping again, afraid if he did he would never be able to start again.

It was another nightmare hike to the lake.

When they reached it, he slid his shoulder down the trunk of a pine tree and leaned against it, closing his eyes. His back throbbed, his side ached, and he just wanted to sleep.

Lydia sat down and leaned against him. He wanted to mumble to her to wrap his coat around her, but he didn't have the strength to do it. He faded away into oblivion.

CHAPTER 11

SOMETIME LATER THE NOISE of a boat engine entered his dreams and someone was pushing his shoulder.

"Wake up, Jack."

He did, surprised he was still alive.

Lydia stood nearby and stared down at him.

"Signal three times with the flashlight," he murmured.

He didn't see what she did, but in minutes strong hands pulled him to his feet, bracing him, nearly carrying him as he dragged his feet down to the boat. The man steadied him when he stepped in and slumped onto a seat. Lydia climbed aboard herself and sat beside him.

Unable to lift his head to look at the man, he remained hunched over.

"Anyone else coming?" asked the driver.

Steel couldn't shake his head.

"No," said Lydia.

The engine started. He was grateful the wind hit his back and not his face. He dozed.

Sometime later they woke him, took the gun off him, and two men helped him climb out of the boat and into the seaplane where he was helped into a seat. He didn't want to move again. He couldn't.

A medic on board removed his jacket and shirt, gave him some morphine, and then proceeded to clean and bandage his wounds, a tortuous process that he suffered through in silence, kept half-awake by the pain.

Finishing up, the medic nodded to him. "You're lucky to be alive. I'm surprised the bear didn't tear your ribs out."

"I had a Cordura sling bag on my back."

"Lucky." The medic draped Steel's torn shirt and jacket over his shoulders, and then put a blanket over his legs and lap.

Next the medic checked Lydia for injuries. Not finding any, he wrapped her up in a blanket in the seat next to Steel.

Lydia curled her legs beneath her and leaned over to rest her head on Steel's lap. She was breathing peacefully in moments. He put an arm around her, his eyelids heavy. He forced himself to remain awake.

"I need to speak to someone about intel," he murmured. The morphine was easing the pain.

The medic nodded and left.

A man wearing a black Lycra hood came back from the front passenger pilot seat, trading places with the medic—who went up front and donned a pair of headphones. Steel guessed they didn't want him listening in.

While Lydia slept, the hooded man sat in front of him, wearing black jeans, a black shirt, and black shoes.

"Phone in my pocket," he murmured.

The man dug it out. "It's ruined. Water."

"Yeah." From memory, Steel gave the three phone numbers to the man, who wrote them down. He explained the liquid VX plan and the information Elias had given about the contacts and passwords, cautioning that the passwords might be warnings. He also mentioned Lydia's aunt in Michigan.

The hooded man said, "Tell me what happened on the Op and how you lost two men."

Steel hadn't expected to be debriefed now and the question caught him by surprise. On the return walk he had no time or energy to prepare his story. It made him wonder what authority the man had. He was also annoyed that the man implied it was his fault Brad and Charlie had died.

"Who are you?" he asked.

The man spoke matter-of-factly. "Colonel Danker sent me. I've decided to debrief you now so you can get better medical attention on the next flight."

He accepted the explanation and sleepily recounted the story of Brad's death, his interrogation of the terrorist, his capture, and Charlie's death. After that he finished the story quickly, leaving out the part of risking the mission to protect Lydia. Instead he said he used Lydia as a means to stay alive and escape, adding that she saved his life by scaring the bear, by killing Adam, and by helping him reach the exfil point.

Without saying anything, the hooded man stared at him for a minute. He finally said in a cool, detached voice, "Tell me again what happened, moment to moment, after Brad died."

Steel looked at him with bleary eyes. "I'm tired."

"I need to hear it again now, while it's fresh."

He became wary, realizing the hooded man didn't believe his story. Very carefully he told the story again, maintaining what he had said the first time. Exhausted, it was easy for him to mumble and nod off at times during the story.

When he finished, the hooded man said, "I want to hear the part about your escape up to killing Elias once more, then we're finished."

Steel stared at the man. "Don't you believe me?"

"You know it's a required part of Blackhood Ops. Thoroughness."

Going even slower, he told the story a third time. He sensed the man either reveled in violence or wanted to catch him in a lie. Either way, Colonel Danker and the hooded man would never be able to verify what had actually happened.

"Did you get attached to the girl?" The man leaned forward. "Did that make you take unnecessary risks?"

Steel didn't answer.

"You have a daughter, don't you?"

Steel glared at him. "How do you know I have a daughter?"

"It's my job to know. Answer the question."

"I stopped a terrorist plot that was much more serious than the smaller action described by Danker in the pre-Op briefing."

"Colonel Danker."

Steel ignored the correction. "Do you think I could have done that if I was worried about saving the girl?" He was concerned the man would try to question Lydia. Then again, he doubted the interrogator had that right or authority.

"The girl puts Blackhood Ops at risk." The hooded man said it factually.

Steel glanced at Lydia's face as she slept on his lap. The only reason he was here was because of her. Anger rose in his throat, but he calmed himself. "She doesn't know anything about me or the terrorists, or what any of this is about."

The hooded man stared at him, his voice sounding clinical. "If it was a family cabin her aunt might have access, or request that the Canadian government look into it to obtain her sister's body."

He thought about that. "Tell the aunt that a man hunting in the woods helped Lydia escape from her parents' killers and leave it at that. The woman might request her sister's body, but she won't want Lydia to relive the event by telling the story to Canadian police, and Canada can't extradite Lydia for questioning. The U.S. government will put up roadblocks to any of it, especially since she's a minor."

The hooded man seemed to consider that. "I have to call Colonel Danker and get his decision."

Steel stared at the hooded man, wanting to put a fist into his face. He kept his voice calm. "Tell Danker there is no decision to make. She goes to her aunt."

The man stared at him a few moments, and then went forward again to radio Danker, once more switching places with the medic. In a few minutes he was back in the chair in front of him, the medic leaving again.

Steel hid his tension with sleepy eyes.

"Colonel Danker says that should suffice. We'll make sure the girl gets to her aunt."

Steel sagged in his chair, relieved.

The hooded man left him and went to the front passenger seat, sending the medic back, while he began relaying information to someone else via a cell phone.

Steel thought of Carol and Rachel, suddenly full of optimism inside. He had his life back. His choice to take the mission had been a success, and if he hadn't gone, Lydia would be dead. He was certain of it. The terrorists would never have left witnesses, and he believed that—given the incomplete intel—no other operatives would have done any better.

He had made the right choice. But he couldn't tell Carol that. He slept.

In an hour—or several, he couldn't be sure—he was shaken awake by the medic. The medic and hooded man helped him off the airplane. Lydia walked in front of him. It was dark but warm outside. Not far away a police car was waiting. A female officer got out of the passenger side, looking at Lydia.

Lydia stopped and turned to Steel.

He painfully knelt in front of her, holding her arms. "You're a brave girl, and whenever you think of your parents, remember how much they loved you. I'll never forget that you saved my life, Lydia. I wouldn't be here without your help."

He paused, digging the compass out of his pocket. "I want you to have this, to remember me by." He pressed it into her hand. Originally he had thought of giving it to Rachel, but Lydia needed it more than his daughter.

Tears streamed down her face and she grasped him tightly. It brought tears to his eyes. He didn't know what mattered more to him, stopping the terrorists or saving the life of one little girl.

The hooded man waited a few yards away.

Steel suddenly became wary. He stood and took Lydia's hand, shuffling with her to the female officer near the police car. He wondered what story had been told to the police, and what they would pass on to Lydia's aunt.

"Where are you taking her?" he asked quietly.

The female police officer touched Lydia's shoulder. "Your aunt has been told everything, and she's very excited that you're going to be living with them."

"Where's that?" He still wasn't convinced this wasn't some type of charade.

"We have a long drive to Michigan." The officer smiled at Lydia. "But we'll stop for food along the way." She opened the rear door and went in, motioning Lydia to follow.

Lydia looked up at him, and he nodded. "Go see your aunt, Lydia. She'll take care of you. You're safe now."

She wiped her eyes and got in, and Steel shut the door, placing his palm against the window. Lydia did the same. He backed away and the police car drove off. It was hard to see her go. He wished there was some way to keep in touch with her. Blackhood Ops would never allow it.

"Satisfied?" asked the hooded man.

"Yeah."

The hooded man helped him walk onto a larger plane that would take him to Langley Air Force Base. Steel wondered who the hooded man was—something about him sent off alarms in his head. The man seemed cold and devoid of empathy. It triggered the desire to be held by Carol and Rachel, and to hold them.

The hooded man disappeared up front.

On the plane a doctor and nurse were waiting for him. After take-off, they had him lie on a cot where they administered local anesthesia, re-cleaned his wounds, stitched him up, checked his ears, and gave him antibiotics. They also wrapped his ribs. He mentioned the water he had gulped from the stream and they gave him something for that too.

When they finished, he remained on the cot, finding it comfortable. He closed his eyes and was asleep immediately.

When they landed at Langley Air Force Base, the nurse woke him. Exhausted, his eyes blurry, he couldn't sit up. She helped him. He groaned with the pain.

The nurse and an attendant assisted him off the plane. He never saw the hooded man again.

They helped him to a waiting black sedan. He was glad. There was no way he could stay awake for the three-hour drive home. He fell into the back seat, and the driver said, "Someone will drive your Jeep to your house tomorrow."

"Thanks." He fell asleep immediately.

Hours later the driver's voice woke him up. The man had opened his door and was leaning in to help him. It took him a few moments to gather himself and prepare for the pain that movement would cause.

Slowly he swung his legs out and pushed to his feet with the driver's help.

There were lights and dark figures moving around the car. It confused him for a few moments until he realized he was standing in front of his house. For a moment he thought it was a welcome back party.

It unnerved him to see tripod lights and dozens of flashlights beaming in the dark, some of them held by neighbors. Abruptly his friend Kergan stood before him, wearing a leather coat, his tall frame shadowed by the light, his silver hair gleaming. Kergan was a retired four-star general and had access to the general that ran Blackhood Ops.

It confused Steel. He swallowed hard as he stared at his trusted friend.

Kergan gently grasped Steel's arms. "They wanted me to be the one to tell you, Jack. Blackhood wouldn't allow contact before this."

Steel opened his mouth, unable to speak at first. "What?"

Kergan grimaced. "They found Rachel's bicycle outside a steep chute leading to a cave. A piece of cut rope was attached to her bike. I've looked at it. Recent rain created a river at the bottom of the shaft. They couldn't even go down to look for her. They found Spinner alive and lying on the ground by Rachel's bike."

Steel gaped at his friend, his knees wobbly. Kergan held him up. Spinner, their big chocolate lab, loved Rachel. The dog would have never have allowed anyone to take her without a fight.

Rachel must have climbed the chute. Because he hadn't trusted her to do easy caves, she had picked a dangerous one to prove herself to him. His fault. He wanted his body in that cave, and Rachel standing in the road.

"Carol needs you, Jack." Kergan gently rested a hand on his shoulder.

Steel somehow couldn't comprehend how he could save a little girl from terrorists on a dangerous mission and yet lose his daughter at home. It occurred to him then that Carol had been right, that deep down he thought he could save everyone, and yet he had failed his own daughter.

Struggling to keep from crying out, he desperately looked for Carol. He spotted her leaving the arms of one of her friends.

He stumbled up to her, reaching out. "Carol."

She grasped him, crying hard. "Oh, Jack."

"I'll look for her," he said. "I'll find her."

****

Weeks later, when he was well enough to investigate the chute, he couldn't find her body. He began thinking that Rachel would have never done the chute by herself. He had trained her repetitively to be cautious.

And some passerby couldn't have just grabbed her. Rachel routinely practiced fighting situations in virtual reality simulations and she practiced self-defense skills almost daily.

Plus there were no sign of a struggle and Spinner had no injuries. Nothing fit.

He became convinced an enemy had taken her. Someone powerful and highly skilled. The only question was why they hadn't contacted him yet.

While sitting at his computer station in the barn, he got a call. No return number. A blocked call.

"Your daughter's okay."

The voice was distorted, most likely by a voice enhancer. Steel couldn't even tell if it was male or female. He froze for an instant. "Who are you?"

The call abruptly ended. Steel stared at his phone. Had someone set this up as a tease for him? Or was this some kind of sick prank call? Or a religious zealot trying to give them hope? He called the FBI.

Later at his desk he began going through every mission he had ever participated in for the Army, and the few private contracts he had carried out for others. He made a list of potential enemies, their contact information, and possible motives. He couldn't come up with an angle with anyone that fit.

****

Two months later he sat in the office of the private investigator the Army had referred him to. Supposedly one of the best in the business. Carol sat beside him, her face strained. The man's fees were high. They would have to dip into their savings and other funds. Steel didn't care what it cost. The FBI and police had come up with nothing and he didn't want to rely on just their skill sets.

Wilcox, the investigator, was ex-CIA, and looked fit and steady. He looked up from a file folder and said, "Jack and Carol, I'll have an answer soon. If the call wasn't a prank, we'll find your daughter." He leaned forward. "I guarantee it." He leaned back. "How certain can we be that Rachel didn't die in the climbing shaft?"

Carol crossed her arms. Steel knew she thought their daughter was dead.

He cleared his throat. "I think it's unlikely. Anything I can do to help?"

Wilcox nodded. "Live your life. It's hard, but don't tear each other apart. No one's to blame. Give us a week."

Steel glanced at Carol. She was biting her lip. She blamed him for being gone when their daughter had gone missing, and she was still blaming him. He never disagreed with her. He was blaming himself. Yet he trusted his intuition in everything, and it told him that Rachel was still alive. He would never give up on her.

That night he got a message to contact Colonel Danker on a secure line.

"We have an Op in hurry up status, Steel. Three days. We have a high-level terrorist target." Danker paused, his voice softening. "I wouldn't reach out to you, except we need your skills, Steel. Our intel says this group is going to hit us hard and thousands will die if they succeed. If it's too much, with your daughter missing, I understand. But other families will be missing their kids and spouses if we don't stop the target."

Steel thought on it. "When do you need me?"

"Tomorrow."

He was going crazy sitting around waiting for Wilcox to call, and he had exhausted everything he could do. Three days.

"Are you in, Steel?"

"I'm in."

* * *

Want to see what happens next to Jack Steel?

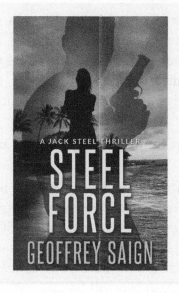

Steel saves a monk from assassins. Now the President, the CIA, and a ruthless billionaire want Steel dead.

SKIP THE FOLLOWING EXCERPT &
BUY STEEL FORCE ON AMAZON NOW.

* * *

AUTHOR'S NOTE

Thank you so much for reading my thriller! In this book I thought it would be interesting to put a Black Ops specialist on a dangerous Op with a victim he wanted to save. I hope you enjoyed reading it as much as I did writing it.

Reviews help me keep writing, and encourage other readers to take a chance on a new author they haven't read before. So if you enjoyed the book, please leave a short review! Every review, even a few words, helps!

Thank you!

~ Geoff

Excerpt from STEEL FORCE

PART 1

OP: KOMODO

CHAPTER 1

Komodo: 2200 hours

MAJOR JACK STEEL'S INTUITION was screaming at him—
things don't feel right!

Everyone at the site was to be terminated, but he
hadn't signed on to murder unarmed civilians. Maybe he just
needed more information. He'd be out of here in two hours.
Home in twenty-four. That's all he wanted, to get home to Carol.
You just have to get through two hours, he told himself.

He clenched his jaw as the plane splashed down on the quiet
waters of the lake. He pulled the black Lycra hood at the back of
his neck over his head so only his eyes and mouth were visible.
Even though his black fatigues were vented, he still sweated
profusely.

Stepping out from behind the massive kapok tree, he waited.

The twin-engine DeHavilland Twin Otter float plane was
almost impossible to see except as a dark shape moving against
the far tree line. Painted all black and gutted for weight so it
could carry extra fuel, it also had no registration numbers on it.

The aircraft angled over to the shore, the engine noise
overwhelming the rainforest sounds until it was cut. A side cargo
door slid open with a rasp and a rope was tossed out.

Steel caught it and pulled the aircraft into the shore, securing the line around a tree. Picking up his silenced SIG Sauer MCX Rattler, he gripped it with both hands. The folding stock made the rifle-caliber machine gun easy to conceal and it had little recoil.

A large hooded figure jumped out of the plane into a few inches of water, also holding a Rattler. Steel recognized the height of the man. Colonel Danker.

"Good to see you, PR." Danker was using Steel's call sign for this mission, *PR*, which stood for *point & recon*. The call sign wasn't very inventive, but Danker had assigned it. Heavily muscled with a gravelly voice, at six-five Danker had three inches on Steel.

"Good to see you, BB." Steel heaved a silent breath, finally relaxing. Danker was U.S. Army and always did things *by the book*, thus his call sign of BB. Steel trusted him.

Everyone else on the Op worked for Blackhood, the private security contractor that signed their checks. But Danker would know all their profiles and made sure they had excellent skill sets for the Op.

Over a year and a half ago Steel had been asked to resign from the Army to join the secret Blackhood Ops program to target terrorists. The missions had been named Blackhood Ops to further distance the U.S. military and put the private military contractor on the hook for responsibility. Except for Danker, the U.S. government wanted no ties to these missions.

Four more hooded men exited the plane, one of them its pilot. Steel didn't know their identities, and they didn't know his—another precaution to maintain Blackhood mission secrecy.

He led them a dozen yards from the shoreline vegetation into the trees, where they squatted in a tight circle.

Each man was equipped with a Rattler, Glock 19, fixed blade knife, and a belt pouch that contained a night monocular scope, first aid, and a GPS tracking unit should things go bad. They also all had small wireless radios, earpieces, and throat microphones. The guns all had their identification numbers erased.

In addition, Steel had a Benchmade 3300BK Infidel auto OTF blade in a small, horizontal belt-sheath built into the inside back of his belt. For his fixed blade he carried a seven-inch Ka-Bar—he liked the leather handle. A small sling bag on his back held rations, a soft-sided canteen, and some first aid supplies.

He looked at Danker. "There are unarmed civilians at the building."

Danker nodded. "Brief us."

From his pouch Steel brought out a piece of white folded plastic and an iridescent red marker. He marked off the position of the site and guard positions.

Glancing around the circle, he said, "Two guards on the roof, two at each of the building's two entrances, four more in the jungle. We'll be coming in due east of the objective. The building has two main wings. Our target will be in the south wing. The target site is in a large clearing, but thick surrounding undergrowth vegetation will give us a lot of cover in our approach."

He showed them the position he would lead them to, then made quick suggestions on how to take out the guards and secure the area and building. Finding optimal strategies was one of his specialties and he didn't expect any objections.

"All civilians should be inside at this time of night." He looked up at Danker.

The colonel said softly, "No warm bodies. No one leaves the site. I'll take care of the primary target. Radio silent unless you're in trouble."

Steel's neck stiffened. He stared at Danker, but the colonel was already upright, waiting. Standing, he whispered, "There are at least four noncombatants at the site, including a Franciscan friar."

Danker spoke matter-of-factly: "Orders stand."

Glancing at the other four sets of eyes, Steel saw only acceptance. "Our drones will record it."

Danker shook his head. "No drones tonight. Take point, PR."

Fifteen years of following orders compelled Steel to nod and move past the others as he returned the plastic and marker to his pouch.

Leading them at a brisk pace through the rainforest, he walked up the gently sloped mountain. The heat produced rivulets of sweat over his torso. His thoughts were racing.

Danker had more intel than he did about the Op and the terrorist. Still, Steel had enough missions under his belt to recognize the difference between uninvolved civilians and those supporting terrorists. The female cook and maid were pushing fifty and were never armed. Like the driver and friar, they didn't act, talk, or move like terrorists in hiding worried about an attack.

He had no problem killing armed guards to get to a terrorist. But his job was to protect civilians, not actively target them. That view had inspired his entire military career. It was the cornerstone of his life.

Danker hadn't even asked how many nonmilitary personnel were on the premises. The colonel didn't care.

Steel's trust in the mission evaporated. Danker was following orders, but Steel questioned the motive of whoever gave them.

He gripped his gun. *No warm bodies*. This wasn't a planned assassination of a known terrorist. It was going to be a massacre.

How could he do anything, when he was the only one who objected?

One against five.

Hell.

CHAPTER 2

Komodo: 2230 hours

S TEEL KEPT MOVING ON the narrow trail, focused on just one thing—surviving the next hour. What sent chills down his arms was that he wasn't sure how far he would—*or could*—go to stop what was coming.

The fluorescent needlepoint of his wrist compass guided him, but he didn't need it. He had traversed this same trail for two nights in a row to make sure he could do it with speed when the time came.

Now he was desperate to know where they were. Over the last three days he heard the guards speak Spanish, but he couldn't place the dialect. They could be anywhere in Central or South America. And the high canopy and the overcast sky prevented any fix on location using stars.

To protect Op secrecy, Blackhood operatives were never given mission locations or terrorist names. Even the GPS unit was rigged so it didn't show numerical coordinates, but they could track him. Real-time tracking via satellites wasn't used on Blackhood Ops to avoid any record and to minimize the number of personnel aware of the Ops.

Except for seeing a photograph of the primary target, Steel knew next to nothing about Komodo Op, other than Blackhood intel indicated the terrorist would be at the termination site for five days.

When he considered the current conflicts and problems, and everyone in power in Central and South America, he concluded they might be in Venezuela. Nicolas Maduro supported Hezbollah and Al Qaeda. Venezuela's embassy had even sold passports to operatives of ISIS.

Maybe Blackhood Ops had decided to take out someone in Venezuela's armed forces that interfaced with terrorists.

That might explain Danker's orders of *no warm bodies*. Even though ISIS had been routed from Iraq, they still had a web presence and there were splinter groups. This might be a preemptive strike to give anyone in the Venezuelan government with terrorist connections a warning: *We can hit you anywhere we want, even in your own country.*

It was the presence of the Franciscan friar that had first triggered Steel's concerns. The diminutive man wore short hair and a brown ankle-length habit with a hood. An image out of the Middle Ages.

Every evening the friar had taken a walk in the forest. Birds flocked into trees near the man. Steel had even witnessed a songbird landing on the friar's shoulder. Amazing. And there was something familiar about the man that Steel couldn't quite grasp.

Once the friar had taken a stroll with the primary terrorist target, who dressed in civilian clothing. Neither were armed. The guards had remained in their positions, seemingly unconcerned about the target's increased vulnerability. That also didn't fit a terrorist camp under heightened security.

In twenty minutes Steel summited the low mountain, and in another ten minutes he led the others down the other side to a large plateau. The building wasn't far ahead. Steel stopped behind a hollow strangler fig tree and held up a hand as he scanned the terrain. He had to estimate where the guards would be, given the lack of light and the waist-high undergrowth that filled in between the trees. The others watched and waited.

A laughing falcon gave its intense *ha-ha-ha-guaco* call in the distance. From much closer came the low-pitched guttural rumbling of a gray-bellied night monkey. Insects buzzed and hummed everywhere. Normally Steel would drink in the teeming life that enveloped his senses. He had a deep abiding love of nature.

But right now he felt trapped.

Shoving panic aside, he focused on his own motto for when a plan blew up: *Stay calm, assess options, look for a solution.* He didn't believe in the Kobayashi Maru principle. He trained in his virtual reality simulations under the belief that there was always a way out of even seemingly impossible situations.

He signaled left and right. The men spread out, Danker to his right. Steel would take the middle, while the others would circle around to the back and sides of the building.

Using the carry strap, Steel positioned the Rattler against his back and lowered himself to his knees, and then his belly. Motionless, he looked ahead for any signs of movement. Crawling around the root buttresses, snakelike, he pressed his hands and arms into the thick detritus. A rich brew of earth filled his nostrils.

He had practiced this part of his plan each day he was here, visualizing the enemy in a position similar to what the guard held now. This was also a maneuver he had repeated a hundred times in his VR sims. Using one foot and arm at a time, he quietly pushed and pulled himself forward. In minutes he spotted the faint outline of the guard sitting on one of the waist-high tree buttresses of a hundred-foot fig tree.

Moving at an angle, he kept crawling until the tree hid him from view.

All the guards wore nondescript tan uniforms and they never changed their nightly positions. Their lack of caution felt amateurish, supporting his doubts about the mission.

He paused at the back of the gnarled tree. No sounds. Methodically he drew himself to his knees, then his feet. Moisture and sweat beaded his face and hands, and the light rainfall patter disguised the quiet whispers of his movements.

Drawing his fixed blade knife, he gripped the handle and slipped over each buttress in turn until only one separated him from the guard. He checked his watch: twenty-three-hundred.

Taking a deep, silent breath, he fluidly slid one leg at a time over the last buttress, allowing his boots to make a slight rustle.

The guard whirled around, wide-eyed.

Steel swung the butt of his knife into the man's temple. The soldier slumped to the ground. Clenching his knife, Steel stared at the limp body. The guard looked young, maybe eighteen. A novice. Not an experienced soldier guarding a terrorist camp.

It cemented his distrust in the mission. Maybe the mission had nothing to do with terrorists. He swallowed. They would be out of here before the guard came to. The risk was that one of Danker's team would discover the man alive.

He picked up the guard's assault rifle, ran forward, and flung it away. Racing through the darkened forest, he slowed when the ranch-style stone building appeared, a lighter shape against the dark forest. Stopping behind a tree, he paused when he heard footsteps.

The friar broke from the surrounding trees in a run, his ankle-length habit flying out behind him as he yelled, "Intrusos! Intrusos!" The small man darted past the startled guards and into the building.

Steel was glad the friar had made it out of the forest without getting shot. He remained behind the tree—he was Danker's backup.

Machine gun fire erupted from several different locations.

Colonel Danker sprinted up beside a nearby tree. He dropped to one knee and sprayed a short burst at the two guards crouched in front of the building. Both men fell to the ground and Danker charged across the open clearing. A guard on the roof leaned over. Danker dove to the ground, rolling toward the building.

Steel stepped out from behind the tree and fired a spray of bullets to cover Danker, his shots much quieter than the staccato bursts coming from the guards around the compound.

The guard of the roof reeled backward.

Rising to his knees, Danker paused only a moment before he rose and ran through the door.

Steel followed at a dead run, adrenaline pumping his legs. More gunfire erupted in the forest. The other guards were fighting back, but he doubted it would help them. The radio silence from the Blackhood team confirmed it.

Steel rushed through the main entryway, past a large living room to the right. No civilians or soldiers. And none of the other Blackhood operatives were inside yet. A short hallway ran left. At the end of it stood Danker, facing a closed door. Steel kept his feet quiet on the stone floor as he ran forward, hoping the colonel didn't look back.

Danker kicked in the door and stepped into the room.

Steel ran harder, his hands like stone on his gun. He heard Danker's gun fire.

He stopped in the doorway just as the colonel swung his machine gun from one corner of the small darkened room toward the other. Steel glimpsed a desk and chair to the left. An interrupted line of bullet holes streaked across the wall behind the desk—it probably hid a corpse—most likely the target.

To the right, over the colonel's shoulder, he saw the friar—his small hands empty, his face hidden in the shadows. Steel snapped a kick into the side of Danker's left knee.

Danker grunted as his knee bent and his back twisted, but he remained upright. He tried to twist around, swinging his gun.

Steel jarred a knife hand into the side of Danker's neck and the colonel collapsed. Adrenaline flooded his limbs and his ears roared as he stared at Danker's crumpled body on the floor. Glancing at the gaping friar, he motioned his gun to the waist-high open window.

The friar's eyes widened, but he ran to it and climbed through.

Steel crossed the room, keeping to the side of the window. He watched the friar disappear in the forest. Shots were fired almost immediately in the direction of the friar's flight. He grimaced. All of it for nothing. And there was nothing he could do for the other civilians. Now he had to worry about his own survival.

He barely whispered, "BB down, south wing."

Danker was unconscious, but a groan came from behind the desk. Simultaneously boots sounded on the stone floor down the hallway.

Steel fired a spray of bullets, aiming high into the forest. Pausing, he turned. A hooded Blackhood operative stood in the doorway, looking down at Danker.

"Let's get him out of here." Steel slung his weapon over his shoulder and hurried to Danker, helping to lift him to his feet. Steel grunted. Danker was heavy.

They half-dragged, half-carried the colonel, who mostly kept his eyes closed. On the way back they all took turns carrying Danker, but it still took an hour to return to the plane. After they loaded the colonel, Steel untied the line, pushed them away from the shoreline, and jumped aboard. The pilot started the engine, sending the smell of burned fuel into the air.

Sitting in a corner, Steel stared at Danker.

The colonel was stretched out on the floor between the others. His hood had been pulled back, revealing his thick black hair, eyebrows, and mustache. Opening his dark eyes briefly, he regarded Steel for a few moments before he closed them again.

There was no light in the plane, but in addition to the pain from a torn knee and screwed-up back, Steel thought he saw hate in Danker's eyes. He also wondered if the colonel sensed the out-of-control feeling sweeping his chest and locking his arms around his knees.

CHAPTER 3

Komodo: debriefing, 0800 hours

STEEL WANTED TO THROW Major Flaut into a wall. But he kept his emotion below the surface and allowed it to evaporate. What had happened on the mission had been shuffled into the background. Now he just wanted to go home to Carol.

He gave a quick upward glance, knowing Flaut would have those blue ice eyes on him, unwavering, cold as his bony face. The man stood over six feet and looked strong, wiry, with nothing that indicated compassion in his manner or words. Probably ex-Special Forces. He wore all black; jeans, turtleneck, and hard-soled shoes.

Flaut would have been assigned by the general running Komodo Op to replace Danker in debriefing. The man was as emotionless as the room they were in.

Steel looked at the bare table, rubbing his forehead with one hand and heaving a sigh, sure the blond-haired Flaut would take it as a sign of weariness. That much was true. He hadn't slept much, instead spending most of the flight preparing his story.

They had flown back to the U.S. in the DeHavilland, first landing briefly somewhere to refuel. Eventually they arrived at a small airfield where all the operatives were separated for debriefing. Steel had waited in the interrogation room for an hour before Flaut arrived. With no chance to shower, he needed fresh clothes and a shave. His uniform reeked.

"Let's go over it again, Major Steel, beginning after you killed the guard."

Steel looked up with a frown. "I ran behind a tree near the target site and saw Danker."

"Colonel Danker."

"Danker killed the two door guards. A guard appeared on the roof. I took him out and then followed Danker in."

"And?"

"I ran in, saw Danker lying in a doorway at the end of a hallway, and ran down. I glimpsed someone outside a window and ran to it." He paused, the image of the friar's face tightening his chest. "I fired, but the person escaped into the forest. Then we dragged Danker out."

"Colonel Danker."

"That's all."

"You didn't see anyone else in the building?"

"No."

"And you didn't see who attacked Colonel Danker?"

"Are you listening?" He glared at Flaut.

"What do you think happened to Colonel Danker?"

"It's obvious, isn't it?" He arched his eyebrows, sensing anticipation in Flaut's stance and his sharp-featured face. The man reveled in this.

Steel focused on Flaut's blue eyes and fair-skinned face. He intuited something else just below the surface. This man could be violent. It was written in his thin lips and taut lines.

"Tell me what's so obvious."

Steel looked down. "Someone in the building surprised Danker."

"Why wasn't Colonel Danker shot?"

He shrugged. "Ask Danker."

"How many other people were in the building?"

"A friar, a cook, a maid, a driver. Maybe a few others. People came and went and I did my reconnaissance at night." That wasn't true. He had used camouflage to observe daytime activities too.

Flaut crossed the small room and sat on a corner of the metal table. He stared from three feet away. Steel didn't look up, but he noted Flaut's smooth movements. Athletic.

Flaut continued. "The other men say that the cook and the maid were the only civilians."

Steel glanced at him. Flaut was lying. They had to know about the friar and the driver. It made him wonder how many others might have been inside the building. His gut tightened. "What happened to the cook and maid?"

"One of the other operatives killed them as they ran out the back door."

"Were they armed?" He locked eyes with Flaut. Tell me that, you SOB. He decided Flaut knew the Komodo Op was a hit squad, probably before he did.

Flaut gave a small smile. "I'm sure they were. You know the mandate for Blackhood missions."

"Covert Blackhood Ops approved by the president to terminate or kidnap terrorists on foreign soil for interrogation and closed trial for crimes committed or planned." He paused. "Noncombatants can be killed only if necessary for mission success, and only if they give primary support to terrorists." He watched Flaut for a reaction, but the major didn't give one.

Flaut pulled out a cigarette, lit it, and took a deep drag. He blew the smoke into Steel's face.

Steel sat back. "Do you mind? There's no smoking."

"Everyone on this Op seems to have a different story, Steel."

"Major Steel to you." He glared at Flaut. "Haven't you ever seen combat? Everyone always has a different story."

A flicker of anger slid through Flaut's eyes "We've been over your map. It looks like you were the closest man to Colonel Danker. It would have made sense that you went in immediately behind him and would have seen his attacker." He blew another cloud of smoke.

Steel had expected this. It was the weakest part of his story. He decided to go on the offensive. "Danker's orders were for no one to leave the site alive." He looked at Flaut. "Those were Danker's orders, weren't they?"

"The mission statement for Blackhood Ops doesn't allow for that. I'm sure you're mistaken."

"Then it sounds like a lot of people might be mistaken about what they saw and heard."

Flaut gave a weak smile. "It was a very capable man who attacked Colonel Danker. There doesn't seem to be a likely candidate."

"How long am I going to be kept here?"

"A few more hours, if you cooperate. You will cooperate, won't you?"

"Sure, as long as you're civil." He gave a plastic smile when Flaut's face darkened. "Look, we're wasting time here, aren't we?" Bunching his shoulders, he leaned forward. "What motive could any of our men possibly have for disobeying orders and attacking a senior officer?"

He waited, knowing Flaut would have no answer, and that if Flaut did have an answer, he couldn't state it. He shook his head. "Had to be someone in the building, one of the target's guards." Sitting back, he waited, knowing he had stated his case as strongly as he could.

Flaut moved off the table and leaned against one of the walls. "Let's go over it a few more times. Maybe something will turn up."

CHAPTER 4

SEVERAL HOURS LATER FLAUT was alone in a small office. He stared through the open door and down the hallway at Steel's receding back—imagining it exploding and spattering the walls in red.

He dialed a number on his phone and said, "You're not sedated?"

"I am but tell me anyway."

"Steel's story holds water. Barely. I'm wasting time at this point so I released him."

"But you think he's lying?"

"Sure."

"He doesn't know that you've been on Blackhood Ops before?"

"No chance."

"Good. I'll take it from here."

Flaut hung up and made another call. To Torr. He had a hunger and he wanted Torr to feed it.

***

Danker put his phone down on the table next to the hospital bed. He bunched his big hands into fists on his white nightgown and clenched his jaw. The Komodo Op had been a complete failure and his reputation had been tarnished. Worse, he had always prized his healthy body, which was now a mess. A cripple for life.

Pillows supported his aching knee, which still had the surgery dressing wrapped around it. His neck felt like it had a spike rammed into it. But he would be out of here in a day or two. The most painful part was that he wanted to put a bullet into Steel—and couldn't. It wasn't legal stateside. Though he wouldn't have hesitated on the Op.

He believed in following the law. Even in the little things like not going over the speed limit. That frustrated people sometimes, but that was okay with him. A few friends were enough. His dad had drilled it into him that if people didn't follow the law, all you had left was chaos.

He had followed orders. And Steel was the only operative who had questioned his command to neutralize everyone at the compound. When Danker considered the assault positions of the other men on the Komodo Op, and the targets at the compound, only Steel would have been close enough to attack him. And only Steel had the ability to surprise him and take him down so fast.

That was part of the reason Steel was always desirable on Ops. He had an uncanny, nearly virtuoso skill set that few could match. The guy was also one messed up SOB.

Questions about Steel's decision-making skills had been raised a year ago in a previous Op, Hellfire, which had caused Danker to wonder about Steel's sense of priorities. At the time he had no proof, and Steel had been heroic. However, Komodo Op confirmed that the man would disobey orders in favor of his own set of values.

Time and planning would bring Steel to him. Being practical and methodical had always served him well. Patience. He would find a way to bring Steel down.

He looked at his aching knee. The doctor said it would never be the same again. He started moving his foot up and down—and gasped in pain.

For the first time in his life he considered breaking the law.

BUY STEEL FORCE ON AMAZON NOW

Read all the Jack Steel and Alex Sight Thrillers.

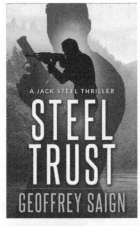

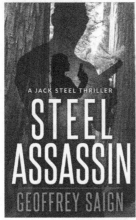
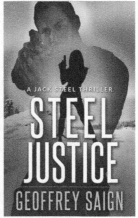
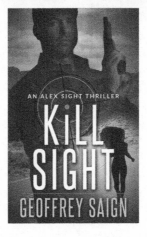

ACKNOWLEDGMENTS

I WANT TO THANK MY friend Stanley Blanchard who used his extensive military background to strengthen the military scenes and give Jack Steel the nuances he needed to play the part. Any mistakes or omissions in anything military is my fault alone. Thanks to Steve McEllistrem, my cousin and fellow writer who gave the book a read for grammar. I also wish to thank my parents for their critiques—they have always had a sharp sense of what makes a great action thriller.

The character Jack Steel follows his values above all else. Doing the right thing is something you learn from the adults around you. My parents did a great job of teaching that to me.

Lastly, I wish to thank all the men and women who act heroically every day to ensure our safety. We owe you our thanks, gratitude, and support.

AWARD-WINNING AUTHOR GEOFFREY SAIGN has spent many years studying kung fu and sailed all over the South Pacific and Caribbean. He uses that experience and sense of adventure to write the Jack Steel and Alex Sight thriller action series. Geoff loves to sail big boats, hike, and cook—and he infuses all of his writing with his passion for nature. As a swimmer, he considers himself fortunate to live in the Land of 10,000 Lakes, Minnesota.

For email updates from Geoffrey Saign
on releases and discounts go to
https://geoffreysaign.net

Made in the USA
Coppell, TX
08 February 2022

73123618R00059